Broken City

www.officialsamwinter.com

ALSO BY SAM WINTER

BROKEN CITY

PRELUDE TO CALAMITY

SAM WINTER

PROLOGUE

DERRICK HART

Derrick leaned forward, feeling the weight of his elbows digging into his knees. Drops of sweat pooled at the end of his short bangs, the bridge of his nose, and his chin before the droplets rained down on the carpet below where he sat.

How much blood, sweat, and tears has this absorbed over the years? He wondered, staring down at the gray carpet below.

The shouting outside was barely audible in the interior roll call room of the central police precinct. That was nice, at least. Derrick's hearing was starting to go out. There was a ringing in his left ear that reminded him of leaving a rock concert. The heavy silence of the room made the ringing even louder.

Fifty police officers were packed inside the room that was meant to only hold half that amount. The twenty-five who hadn't managed to secure a chair for the brief break they enjoyed leaned against the walls or sat on the floor in a defeated pile of limbs and eighty pounds of riot gear. Derek pulled both layers of his body armor down from his neck and felt the hot air trapped against his chest rise, happy to have a place to escape. His undershirt clung to his body like he had just worn it into the pool, but at least he got some fresh air in there to try and cool down.

"You know, I was supposed to be in Memphis right now," Hughes said.

He was sitting in the seat beside Derrick. His thirty-pound heavy vest was sprawled on the table before him, along with a few random pieces of riot gear armor he'd stripped off as soon as he sat down: one shoulder pad, two forearm pads, and one glove.

Derrick looked up, realizing the man was talking to him.

"I got this week of vacation approved on freaking January 1st. Four months ago." Hughes shook his head. His sweat-soaked shirt revealed the start of a round beer belly. Hughes was a giant, though, so when he stood the belly somehow disappeared into his frame. "I should be stuffing my face with some dry rub barbecue, sittin' by the pool, knockn' back Bud Lights right now."

Hughes finished his third bottle of water like he was chugging a beer. "Instead, I'm here. Doing this shit."

Brennan scoffed behind them. "Bud Light?" Brennan's eyes narrowed on the rest of the officers listening in. "Why the fuck would you drive all the way to Memphis just to drink water?"

A small laugh rose through the room. It was an exhausted laugh.

"Tonight's my ten-year wedding anniversary," another man said at the front of the room.

"Dodged that bullet!" the men laughed at someone's comment.

"Are you kidding? You know he's going to get it as soon as he gets home," Brennan joked. "Best just pull a double tonight. At least you can arrest people when they yell at you."

"I already pulled a double," the first guy said bitterly. "Working on my triple right now."

"Hey, you never know. Maybe she lets him use his hand-cuffs on her?"

The room came alive as the officers clung desperately to whatever levity they could. Derrick laughed with them and enjoyed being a spectator, not having to turn his brain back on yet. They knew their break was almost over.

Derrick caught eyes with an older officer with a paunch and a thick mustache who stood beside Brennan. Derrick didn't know the man's name, but he had seen him many times over the years in passing. The man leaned from side to side, often shifting weight, and seemed to be hurting more than most. Pointing at his seat and nodding at the officer, Derrick stood when the bigger man gave him a grateful smile and a pat on the shoulder as he took Derrick's seat. Derrick grabbed his ballistic helmet and moved to the wall.

"Five-minute warning," Sergeant Downs said while looking at his watch.

The room went quiet after they each took turns releasing exasperated sighs.

Derrick used his last minutes to stretch. His calves, his back, his quads... all the muscles that had grown stiff and cramped over the past hours on the line.

Hughes looked over his shoulder, "Hey, Hart, why don't you take that cannon of yours and fire a few grenades into the street already? What are ya waiting for?" Hughes nodded at the small, single-shot grenade launcher that was slung behind Derrick's back.

"And ruin all this fun we're having?" Derrick smirked as he twisted his back and heard a crack.

"He's just going after that overtime," Brennan mused. The round eyes and constant smile the man wore gave him a look similar to that of a Labrador Retriever.

"Good god, man. When this week's check hits, it's going to be historic," Derrick said.

Brennan nodded, "A few more nights like this one and I think the police department will single-handedly bankrupt the city on OT."

"Fuck, don't jinx us," Hughes waved a hand over his head. "I can't do another night of this shit."

Derrick thought about what he would do with his overtime money. The obvious choice was to pay off the five-thousand-dollar credit card bill he racked up.

Or you could just return the fucking engagement ring...

Derrick let his mind wander to Alyssa for a moment. To how this was the longest they had gone without speaking since they started dating years ago. She might have already fled the city. Maybe she went to her parents' place. He quickly shook away the thought, having already broken his promise not to think about Alyssa.

"You know," the big man who took Derrick's seat spoke, "I was supposed to be at Disney World this weekend."

The room went silent, then a chill went down Derrick's spine as he remembered the latest video footage released from the Florida hot zone.

"Well, that's drawing the long straw if I ever heard of it," Brennan said.

"Yeah, you ain't kidding," the man replied. "Can you imagine if I'd scheduled the family trip last weekend instead and been there when the infection hit?"

"Go buy a lotto ticket, ASAP," Derrick added.

"Break's over, ladies and gents," Sergeant Downs announced. "Get your gear on and grab a water bottle for the road. Could be a bit before we get relief."

The roll call room became a living organism with fifty different appendages all moving at once. They strapped on armor, finished protein bars, and single-serving bags of chips, and filtered out the doorway to the exit. No one wanted to go back out there. But it was their job. Their duty. What kind of person would they be if they fled when duty called?

"Why grab an extra bottle of water? I'm sure if you're thirsty, they'll be happy to throw one to you," a woman joked as she joined the single-file line.

Derrick grabbed two bottles from the torn, open case of water as he passed it. Down the hall and to the front door of the precinct, he could hear the shouts grow louder as he neared. Like honing in on a fight in a crowd of people, the curse words became intelligible as the intensity grew. The thick blanket of humidity that fought its way inside the air-conditioned precinct covered Derrick a few feet from the doorway.

He settled his ballistic helmet on top of his head and cinched the chin strap on tight. Pulling the plexiglass visor down, Derrick left the precinct and entered the chaos of downtown Birmingham. One hundred and ten police officers surrounded the Central Police Headquarters standing shoulder to shoulder. And surrounding them were twenty-five thousand rioters, their bodies clogging the streets in every direction. Their screams blurred together into a wall of rage—just another day at work.

ONE

DERRICK HART

Working the front line of a violent protest without barriers was like being in a fight, only you had multiple opponents, and the rules were constantly changing. Also, you were the only one who had to follow the rules.

Protests had been popping off across the city the past couple of nights, ever since the nationwide curfew and mandated shelter-in-place order was issued by the President of the United States. They grew more violent each day, it seemed, but they all blended together for Derrick. The bruises he wore the next morning all felt the same.

Every major city in the United States faced protesting ever since video footage of the outbreak flooded twenty-four-hour news channels and social media. The infection was worse than COVID-19. It was worse than Ebola. It was violent. Government officials hadn't named it yet, but the internet had, of course.

Rabid had been making the rounds for a couple of days now after a doctor on a popular podcast compared it to rabies, but far worse. It was hyper contagious and killing the entire state of Florida. The southern cities like Birmingham had to contend with mass migration to the north on top of the protesting, but the looting and riots had been worse in the larger cities in the north like Chicago and New York City.

Derrick stood at the top of the stairs and peered out over the sea of shouting faces glaring at him. He watched the bodies mash into one another. An eerie wave moved through the crowd as they all pushed against one another. It was a beautiful cacophony. Something between a mosh pit and a stampede. Police had dispersed the crowds before they grew to the level of riots so far, but...

"Maybe tonight will be the night," Derrick mumbled to himself.

"Huh?" Sergeant Downs shouted as he clapped his helmet's faceplate against Derrick's to hear better.

"Nothing!" Derrick shouted back.

"Keep that launcher close. We might need it tonight!" Sergeant Downs jabbed his finger towards Derrick's leg where the launcher dangled.

Derrick nodded his helmet, then smacked at the grenade launcher he had slung over his shoulder and clipped to the back of his body armor with a carabiner clip. Sergeant Downs smacked his shoulder and moved down the line to where a skirmish was breaking out between an officer on the front line with a shield and four protesters shoving into him.

Derrick Hart was an average-looking, almost thirty-year-old man. With brown hair and a plain face, he didn't stand out in a crowd. That was fine; he enjoyed blending in. In uniform, however, it was easy to see he was different. While every other police officer wore navy blue uniforms so dark they looked black, the uniform Derrick wore was forest green. The back of his chest armor read 'SWAT' in bold white letters so supervisors could readily identify him in an emergency. He was the last resort.

Derrick was on the arrest team tonight. He and the five other members of his team stood behind the double lines of officers that kept the protesters at bay.

There was a sudden surge in the crowd about twenty yards to the right that pushed their officers back a step. The achievement riled the protesters nearest it like they had found progress after hours of stagnation. One of the front-line officers' shield was ripped right from his grasp, and a second later the officer was tugged into the ocean of protesters.

"Over there!" Derrick pointed as he started running.

"I see it!" Brennan replied and followed.

Derrick looked over his shoulder and saw Sergeant Downs at the opposite corner of the building dressing down an officer. Pressing the receiver on his radio mic, Derrick yelled, "First and seventeenth! Officer down! Officer down!"

The noise was too loud. He couldn't even hear his own voice. Who knew if others could? Empty cans and trash flew over the line of officers where they ran. A full bottle of water slammed into the side of Derrick's helmet and staggered him off balance. He swiped the floating trash bag out of his sight as he reached the section of officers battling the worst of it.

The fellow officers to the right and left of the patrolman who was taken pushed at the crowd with their shields, trying to find their brother-in-arms, but the protesters punched and kicked at their shields in response. They swung on the officers with gnashing teeth and faces glistening with sweat. It was a release of aggression, like they were working a punching bag. Only it was an officer they struck, not a leather bag.

"Move, move!" Derrick ordered as he pushed to the front of the line.

"Hart, what are you doing?" Hughes yelled as he crowded behind Derrick with the rest of their arrest team.

Derrick shoved his way into the battle of bodies with squinted eyes. Even if Derrick was as big as Hughes, the power of the crowd felt like a violent storm raising twenty-foot waves that knocked the largest man where they wanted. The fists, bottles, rocks, and cellphones hammered his helmet and created a percussion of sounds that echoed in his ears. Cellphone lights shoved in his face illuminated clenched teeth and snarling faces in the crowd. His ribs were struck from the right and fingers dug into his left arm, ripping him off balance.

He had made it five feet into the layers of people, and he didn't see the officer. No uniform, body armor, nothing. Derrick even tried to jump to see if he could see the helmet protruding over the others' heads, but five hands smacked at his helmet, keeping him down.

There was a swift and violent yank at the rear of his body armor that nearly ripped the armor off his chest. The heels of his boots dragged across the cement as he watched the small slice he made in the people close as he was extracted.

"Are you fucking crazy?" Hughes bellowed once the big man had dragged Derrick back behind the first line of officers. His voice was lost in the thousand others that screamed.

He still had a grip on Derrick's vest carrier strap on the back of the armor. Hughes was built like a bear just before hibernation and roared like one too when angry.

"Where is he? Did we get him? I didn't see him." Derrick looked from Hughes to Brennan and the other officers on the line, and they all shook their heads. Leaving the crowd of people was like breaking through the surface of the water in a hurricane. The violence was disorienting.

"What the hell is going on?" Sergeant Downs asked, slowing from his run to their position.

"An officer on the front lines. He was taken," Brennan pointed. "Pulled into the crowd. We can't find him."

Wide-eyed and searching, Derrick paced the line back and forth looking for a way in.

Sergeant Downs was on his radio while doing the same. "Code 8000! Code 8000! Officer down! First Ave N and Seventeenth Ave N! All available—"

Derrick clicked on his flashlight and saw only more angry faces and middle fingers shoved in his direction. Dropping to a knee he fell over from how unbalanced he was in the armor but shined his light between the feet and saw nothing.

Just legs. Just fucking legs! Where did he go!?

"Wait! There! Right there! Shit," Derrick cursed and struggled to his feet. "I see him. He's on the ground getting trampled or beat up—I don't know."

"Where is he exactly?" Sergeant Downs leaned closer to Derrick and Derrick pointed to a section that was about ten yards to the right of where the man was taken and five yards deep. Downs nodded, then shouted to the second row of officers, "Arrest formations! Arrest formations!"

"Get ready guys!" Derrick yelled at the rest of the arrest team. Hughes instinctively took point at the front of the charge. Brennan moved to his left, Derrick went to his right, and the three others filled in behind them. "Hughes, time to let out that missed Memphis barbecue aggression."

"You're goddamn right," he replied. His voice sounded more like a growl.

The loudest and most violent protesters at the front of the crowd saw them preparing to enter their territory and amped themselves up. Two men pulled off their shirts and wrapped one of their knuckles with it as they got into a boxer's stance.

Derrick tried to close his mouth and force himself to control his breathing through his nose. The fear, excitement, and adrenaline narrowed his field of vision to the suspects directly in front of them. He tried to work some spit in his mouth, but there was none to be found.

Sergeant Downs backed to the side after giving instructions to the front two rows and held up a single hand, "Arrest formation! Deploy! Deploy! Deploy!"

The first line of officers parted like the Red Sea as a dozen more from the second line charged ahead, followed by the arrest team. Derrick felt bad about the officers ahead of Hughes. They had made it three or four yards into the crowd before the thousands of people stopped their momentum. The two wannabe boxers punched, grabbed, and pulled at the shields, but they were flattened against the people behind them. Hughes' solution to the stagnation was to grab hold of the biggest officer in front of him and use him as a shield to batter his way to the last steps. Derrick did his best to hold his own on the right flank, but ultimately everyone was knocked into Hughes' wake.

Hughes was just to the left of the taken officer, and charged by him three steps before realizing it. Derrick saw the fallen officer's feet first, then, as the people that stood over him with their camera phones out bled away, they left a lone, wiry man standing over the officer and stomping down on the officer's chest.

Derrick led with his fist. The man had his knee raised for another stomp when the punch connected just beneath his eye. The suspect stumbled backward, and Derrick followed. Derrick tripped over the officer just as his second punch smashed into the suspect's nose.

The suspect curled to his side and covered his face as Derrick kneeled over him with a third punch readied but halted it after he saw the threat was stopped. Looking up, Derrick saw a dozen people charging at him, and he considered curling into the fetal position himself before the feet began to stomp down on him.

Then backup arrived.

The dozen officers fought their way to him and encircled the arrest team, giving them room to work. They were now a lone circle of eighteen officers surrounded by an angry mob of thousands. A tiny eye of calm in the hurricane.

Hughes and Brennan fell on top of the suspect and yanked his hands away from his bloody nose, getting to work with the handcuffs. Derrick crawled back to the fallen officer. He was a smaller guy. Probably five foot three. The riot gear on one side of his body had been torn away. His uniform was ripped, but his gun was still in its holster.

"Are you okay, man? Can you hear me?" Derrick shouted.

The officer's visor was shattered, but the helmet was still on, which had probably saved his life.

"I—yes," he said.

"Are you hurt bad? Can you walk?"

"I don't—my leg hurts," the man said, holding his left knee.

Derrick nodded. "Okay, use the other one. We got to get you on your feet and out of here."

The circle that the twelve officers had claimed for them had quickly shrunk in the few quick seconds that had passed. Derrick could almost touch all twelve of the officer's backs that protected them.

"Brennan!" Derrick called.

"Yeah, we're ready!" he replied. He and Hughes each held an arm of the handcuffed suspect, who teetered on his feet.

Derrick pulled the injured officer to his feet in an awkward bear hug. The man cried out, then swallowed the rest of his pain as he leaned on Derrick's shoulder.

They started the slow and suffocating process of pushing back to the police precinct. Hughes maneuvered to the front with the suspect in hand. The suspect didn't enjoy the violent crowd as much as he had before and was ducking his head behind the officers for protection. They spilled out of the people and stumbled back to the safety of police headquarters. Two officers were standing by to escort the injured officer inside for medical treatment, while two others took the suspect to a holding room.

"Good work, Hart," Sergeant Downs started to say, but fights were breaking out along the entire line. The protest was over. The crowd wanted a riot now.

There was a high-pitched whistle followed by a rush of wind as a bottle rocket fired between Derrick and Sergeant Downs narrowly missed them both and exploded on the building. They both ducked as three more fired off in their direction.

"Are you kidding me?" Sergeant Downs said. "We're done with this shit. Use the launcher."

"Lieutenant Tomlen signed off on it?" Derrick asked.

"I'm fuckin' signing off on it," Sergeant Downs said as he ducked another bottle rocket. "Yeah?"

Derrick smirked and nodded in agreement.

"Line two! Line two! Don gas mask! Don gas mask!" the Sergeant announced down the line.

The word was spread around the building while Derrick went inside to grab the small satchel of tear gas grenades. By the time he returned outside, all the officers had their gas masks on.

Derrick grabbed his mask from his pouch, placed it to his face, pulled the mesh webbing behind his head, and cinched the straps beneath his chin. A firework mortar launched at the front door. There was a brief pause that allowed Derrick to dive out of the way before it detonated in bright, beautiful reds and oranges that burned every officer they touched. The glass windows surrounding the door were shattered.

If they land one of those shots inside the building, they could burn it down.

Cracking the barrel of the single load launcher down, Derrick loaded a 40mm tear gas canister into the tube and locked it shut. Arching the launcher to the center of the road to his left, Derrick fired the first round. Within seconds of its landing, the smoke bloomed from it. Immediately, Derrick loaded a second and fired it in the opposite direction. By the time he fired the third one, the plumes of tear gas were merging and engulfing the street.

Gaps formed in the crowd as hundreds ran in every direction. Already, the front line of violent protesters wavered. Without the masses at their backs for support and the promise of anonymity, those who threatened officers and sought violence a few minutes ago shrank away into the street. Sergeant Downs spun his finger in the air at Derrick and he fired another three tear gas canisters in the direction the protesters congregated.

The streets cleared and quieted to an eerie silence as the tear gas reached the officers. A handful of officers who didn't have a good seal on their gas masks stepped offline and retreated into the police precinct to fix their masks, but other officers took their places.

Derrick breathed slowly through his mask and steadied himself. He knew this was just the beginning, not the end.

TWO

AARON VANDERKAMP

"It's happening! I mean, like for real! A fucking zombie apocalypse!" Brad only mouthed the curse word, as their parents were frequently pacing in and out of the living room where the three brothers sat.

"They're not zombies," Michael replied. The stack of junk mail he had before him was a wrinkled mess from his incessant folding, unfolding, and refolding in a different way. "They're infected, that's all—just people infected with a virus. No different than if they had COVID-19 or the flu."

"Uh, it's pretty freaking different than if they had the flu, Mike," Brad retorted.

Michael chucked a balled-up piece of cardboard touting 'high-speed internet for a low low price!' The beam of the flashlight between them caught the cardboard striking Brad between the eyes and bouncing comically into Aaron's lap.

"Ah! You fuck-head!" Brad snapped, rubbing his forehead with his fingertip.

"Brad..." their mother spoke with a warning in her tone. She might've been in a different room, and the three boys were all adults or near adults, but that voice was enough to silence them.

Michael and Aaron both snickered as Brad clenched his teeth shut. Aaron watched Brad measure his options, which included leaping over the purple ottoman that separated the three brothers and tackling Michael. But Michael was nineteen years old, the eldest of the three and the biggest. It had been some time since he left high school and last wrestled, but Aaron thought Michael could still beat his seventeen-year-old brother, Brad. Michael eyed Brad, daring him to the challenge. He rubbed his five o'clock shadow, which was almost thick enough to make up a beard, as if underscoring his age advantage. When Brad's face softened and he went back to his game of solitaire, the mood relaxed in the room.

"What about Aunt Kendra?" Aaron asked.

Michael furrowed his brow, "What about her?"

"She's in Brazil right now on a teach-abroad thing. Maybe we can go to her. Probably safer there," Aaron said.

"Heck no," Brad replied. "I ain't going to Brazil, stupid. Cartels will cut Americans into pieces. I'd rather take my chances with the zombies."

"Cartels are in Mexico, genius," Aaron replied.

Brad looked at the doorway leading to the dining room where their parents sat, then back to his little brother and gave him the finger. Aaron just smiled and shook his head. At fifteen, Aaron was the youngest of the three brothers, but he was already an all-American wrestler, a feat that neither of his older brothers had accomplished in their high school wrestling careers. They were less eager to wrestle with him than with each other. No one wanted to be pinned by their little brother.

Their dad stormed to his bedroom, through the living room, and returned with a rifle in hand.

"Dad?" Aaron said.

"It's happening," he announced. "I can see them down the street. The street's full of them!"

"Who is?" their mother asked.

"Looters, vandals, murderers... Who knows?!" their dad shouted.

"John, don't say that in front of the children," their mother whispered, but the three boys were already on their feet and looking out the window.

They couldn't see much at night without the streetlights working, but the moonlight was enough to see shadows of figures jumping and running in the middle of the road.

"They ain't children anymore," their dad said.

"Listen," Aaron said, focusing on his hearing. "It sounds like they're playing music or—"

"Dammit, boys! What'd I tell ya 'bout wasting the flashlight? Turn it off!" his dad said as he stormed back into his bedroom.

Their father had been on edge more than anyone Aaron knew since the start of the outbreak. The conspiracy theories resonated with him more than most. It didn't help that many of his coworkers had been pushing him in that direction for years. He'd worked as a trucking parts salesman for the last twenty-five years, and more than a few of his long-time customers loved to chat about the moon landing being fake, the Earth being flat, and now how this outbreak was a black flag operation. A consolidation of power as the 'deep state' government released the virus on its people to cull the population and gain a greater foothold.

"This is the second phase," his father would rant during the commercials between news programs. "Phase two after 9/11. This new bill will give them even more power; ten times worse than the Patriot Act!"

When the outbreak in Florida was first announced a few

days back, it seemed far away, like a terrorist attack in Europe or the Middle East. Aaron still went to the gym with Brad every day, he still played video games with his friends, and his mom shopped for groceries. His friends talked about the *Rabid* infection much like Brad did—like the zombie apocalypse dream scenario. How each of them would buy machine guns, samurai swords, and duct tape, and be able to outlive everyone else in the world.

Then a day went by, and the internet became too sluggish to play games. Another day passed, and texts stopped sending and cellphone calls sometimes didn't connect. Landline phones were still reliable for the few who still had them. Aaron's mother was among those who hated cell phones. But now the rolling blackout shut all the power off for unknown amounts of time and made the distance between Birmingham Alabama, and Miami Florida seem all the shorter. This was real now.

Brad clicked off the flashlight and put it back down on the ottoman. Aaron could see their mother sitting in the dining room. A single candle illuminated the Bible she had been reading for hours.

"Michael, come and take this," their dad said from the bedroom.

Michael left the room and returned with an AR-15 rifle.

"Brad—"

"John, what are you doing?" their mom asked.

She was on her feet now and shuffling towards the bedroom. Her heart-shaped face and petite body appeared frail when she was afraid, like she had aged twenty years in the last days.

Brad emerged from their parents' bedroom with their dad's hunting rifle and wore a devious grin as he looked through the scope. "Yeah, sniper rifle. I always played the sniper class."

"Don't aim that in the house," their mother scolded as she passed him.

Aaron was left with excitement that he was next to get issued a gun, and terror that if he had a gun, he might have to use it. There was a brief argument between their parents. The hushed whispers of their mother were followed by thunderous shouts from their father. It was nothing new to the brothers. Their mother never got anywhere with her complaints. While they all loved and respected their mother, they all feared their father. He might have been a shorter man, but his stocky frame, hard-ass attitude, and powerful voice gave him a larger-than-life persona.

With a huff of defeat, their mom shuffled back towards her candle and Bible, mumbling to herself. "Well, if you think it's necessary, but I don't think it is."

"Aaron!" his dad called.

Aaron entered his bedroom and saw his father standing over his bed. A small electric lantern lit the open closet door. Boxes of ammunition were piled on the bed, along with a suitcase and clothes. His father pulled back on the slide of his silver pistol and let the spring rack it forward. He offered the grip of the gun to his teenage son. Aaron took the pistol, holding it away from his body like it was a bomb.

"This ain't a toy, understand?" his father growled.

"Yes, sir," Aaron said.

"Don't point it at anyone unless you mean to shoot them."

"Yes, sir," he repeated.

His father went back to counting ammo boxes and Aaron took that as a dismissal. When he left the bedroom, his brothers paid him little attention aside from cursory glances to make sure the youngest hadn't gotten a cooler gun. Michael loaded and unloaded the magazine in his rifle while practicing shouldering the weapon like he was a soldier. Brad aimed his scope down the road towards where the looters were. Aaron just kept his pistol by his side. They all had gone shooting with their father, of course. They were familiar with all his guns. Brad had even gone deer hunting with him once, which was probably why he got the hunting rifle. But they didn't have guns for hunting now.

"Dad, there's more of them," Brad said. "On the other side of the block."

"Where?" their dad shoved between Brad and Michael, looking out the window.

"Oh, John, don't let them point those things out the window. Someone is going to think we're crazy people," their mom said, and their father smacked Brad's rifle down from where he aimed.

The street had groups of people gathered now at the inter-sections on both sides. Shadowed bodies jumped and danced around cars that thumped music throughout the neigh-borhood.

"They look like teenagers," Aaron said.

"Doesn't mean anything," Michael said.

"That's right; they're still dangerous," his father agreed.

"Why are they out so late? Don't they know about the curfew?" his mother whispered. Aaron felt her hands on his shoulders as she peered over them.

The cars started doing donuts in the intersection nearest them, and the people began to scatter to avoid the four cars that screeched in circles. Six of the teenagers ran into their front lawn, and Aaron saw his father's jaw tighten.

"Nancy, call the police. Get them on the phone now," his father barked, and Nancy shuffled back to the dining room, where the cordless landline phone sat in the corner.

"But they're just standing there, Dad," Aaron said.

"Who cares?!" Brad shoved Aaron's shoulder. "That's our

lawn. Let me go out there and scare them, Dad. Come on. I'll just fire a warning shot at their feet."

"Give me that!" His father yanked the rifle away from Brad and set it down on the ottoman. "You don't shoot unless your brother does, and he doesn't shoot unless I tell him to. Now get away from the windows."

The six in their yard grew to ten, huddling in a circle and passing a bottle of liquor amongst themselves. Their laughs and shouts carried through the windows into the house and agitated their father.

"Nancy?"

"They won't answer!" their mother sounded beyond flustered. She had been tapping her fingers nonstop on the dining room table for fifteen minutes. "It just says the same recorded message that all dispatchers are busy and—"

"They're heading to our backyard, Dad," Michael whispered. He jogged low with his rifle shouldered to the back door. Aaron followed, worried about what was about to happen.

This isn't a 'gun' situation, right? Why do we need guns right now? he thought.

Three teenagers had hopped their chain-link fence and entered their backyard. They stumbled around Aaron's mother's garden for several minutes and laughed as they booted her gnomes.

"Stop that!" his mother yelled a whisper, as if the teenagers could hear.

She bounced in her seat with her cell phone to her ear. Twenty-seven minutes on hold with 911.

It wasn't until one of the men picked up one of the smaller gnomes and threw it against the back sliding glass door that his father went outside.

"Stay inside, stay hidden. Only come out if I tell you to, you understand?" he said to Michael, who nodded.

"John, what are you doing?" their mother stood, panic vibrating in her voice. "Wait for the police—John!"

But their dad was already opening the sliding door. He left his rifle leaning against the inside of the house so the three trespassers couldn't see it. The muted laughter and distant music suddenly filled the quiet house.

"Hey! What do you think you're doing?" he yelled, stepping out onto the back deck. The three boys went silent for a quick beat, then continued their laughter.

"Shut the fuck up, man," one of them replied.

"Yeah, go back inside, bitch. We'll tell you when we're finished," another added.

Aaron winced, already seeing in his head where this conversation was going. He looked down at his father's rifle and considered grabbing it before this escalated to him doing something that might land him in jail.

"Who are you calling a bitch?" his dad spat. "Get off my property before I beat your fucking asses!"

"Fuck you," the third man cursed.

"You want to fucking fight, bitch?" their voices moved closer.

"Oh, I'm going to get that ass!"

Aaron heard the footsteps thunder up the steps to the deck as his dad ran inside and grabbed the rifle. Aaron yelled for his dad, but the gunshots muted all sounds. He wasn't sure how many his father fired, but when it was over, Aaron had his left hand pressed against his left ear and the butt of the pistol in his right hand pressed to his right ear.

His mom was crying. Aaron's right ear rang and dulled the yelling between his father, Brad, and Michael. Aaron saw shadows running towards the street and heard car tires screech as they peeled away.

"Nancy, get the police," his dad said. He moved from

window to window of the house, making sure they weren't being surrounded or someone else was hiding on the side of their house.

Aaron shuffled beside Michael, who stood in the sliding glass doorway with his rifle aimed at the deck stairs. A teenage boy lay at the bottom of the stairs. His legs were folded awkwardly beneath his body. He didn't move.

"Nancy! Get the fucking cops here!" his dad demanded as he returned to the sliding glass door.

"I'm still on hold!" his mother cried.

THREE

DERRICK HART

Derrick's legs dangled out of the driver's window of his Charger. Socks and boots were off and hung out the passenger window to dry while he slept. The blisters on his heels needed fresh air anyway. Derrick hadn't bothered showering or tending to his newest collection of bruises and cuts before passing out—an error he would come to regret, he was sure, later that day.

By the time Derrick and the other officers had cleared streets, transported and documented their arrests, and documented their use of force for the media department to do their press release, it was five-thirty in the morning. Lieutenant Tomlen wanted Derrick to complete three separate incident reports: one for the injured officer, one for the suspect he'd punched, and another for launching the tear gas. The LT hadn't been happy that no one asked his permission first.

Derrick politely told the Lieutenant, "Hell no."

Then Sergeant Downs less politely said the same thing.

SWAT was short-staffed—hell, everywhere was short-staffed nowadays. Downs had told him in passing that there were thirty-five 'no-call, no-shows' last night, and that was on top of the twelve the day before. Police officers could read the writing on the walls and were quitting in droves. They saw the infected in Florida tearing people apart like a pack of wolves. Every officer in the country knew if the infected reached their city, they would be on the front lines.

Derrick was on permanent on-call status, as he was one of eight SWAT-certified officers left in the city. He had meant to go home, let his dog out, shower in his own shower, and sleep in his own bed.

That didn't happen.

Instead, he snored in the front seat of his car with his neck craned against the rifle rack between the two seats. Strange nightmares of black goo tortured him. Thick molasses, as dangerous as quicksand, devoured his limbs one at a time and was about to cover his mouth when he was startled awake.

"Hey buddy... have a good nappy nap?" Adams asked.

Derrick took an extra second to scramble his legs inside the vehicle and remember his surroundings and where he was in life. He felt the beat of his pulse pounding along the side of his throat, and the start of a sticky layer of sweat building on his forehead. It was going to be a humid day.

"Oh, damn, it was one of those good sleeps, huh?" Adams said.

They were in the South-East precinct back parking lot. A twelve-foot-tall chain-link fence surrounded them with razor wire lining the top of it—the only place a cop could feel safe sleeping in their car.

Derrick cleared his throat, "What time is it?"

"Uh, ten-oh-five."

"Then yeah, Adams, that was a great four and a half hours of sleep. Thanks." Derrick scrubbed his face awake and grabbed at his water bottle. "How the hell are you so chipper? No way you got much more sleep than me."

"Six hours. Just what the doctor ordered. And he also ordered some iced coffee," Adams grabbed a large, iced coffee from the roof of Derrick's Dodge Charger and, in a circular motion that he turned into a dance, he handed the drink to Derrick.

"Ah... Some days, Adams, I don't know whether to kill you or give you a hug."

"What about today?"

Derrick cracked the lid off of the drink and took two long gulps, allowing the caffeine to permeate his system and the frozen chunks of ice to melt down the back of his throat.

"Ask me after I finish my coffee."

Adams laughed as he stretched between the two of their vehicles. He was only a few years younger than Derrick, but he was the newest teammate added to the Birmingham SWAT team. He was an excellent officer and a solid SWAT guy. He knew his tactics, and he didn't have an ego. Once Derrick could wear the kid's cheery morning optimism off, he might make for a good drinking buddy.

"You hear about this Honor Bound bill Congress is voting on tomorrow? Blackmailing cops and doctors and all into doing their jobs to save their families? Heard they're calling it a suicide contract for us to sign."

Derrick nodded. "I heard about them. I guess they're getting a lot of no-call, no-shows across the country. You gonna sign?"

Adams shrugged while in the middle of shadowboxing an imaginary opponent. "What for? I don't have no wife or kids. And all my family is already in Arkansas. What about you? You're not married, right? Any kids?"

"No, nothing," Derrick said. He took another sip of his coffee and checked his phone for any calls from her.

"Yeah! Single's the way to go now more than ever, man.

Government doesn't have shit to hold against you. Still, I don't think I'm going anywhere. This week has been an eye-opening experience. Fired the launcher last night at North precinct. I heard you did, too, at Central. Crazy."

"So you're not running for the hills and saying fuck you to the police department like everyone else?" Derrick raised an eyebrow.

Adams made a face and shook his head.

"Why not?" Derrick asked, sipping his coffee.

Adams held his hands out, displaying the badge on the breast of his uniform as if he was a model, "Cause this is what we do."

Derrick snickered and nodded, "This is what we do."

"But... wait, you're dating a girl, aren't you? Alyssa, right?"

Nothing.

"Uh, kinda."

"Kinda? What the fuck's kinda?"

Derrick looked at his phone's background image: a drunken, blurry-faced selfie of him and Alyssa after a night of drinking. Her blond hair draped over part of her face.

"Uh, what? I don't know. We're kinda on a break. I don't know," Derrick said, putting away his phone.

"Oh, my bad. Bad timing for her, though. Bet she comes begging for you back once the National Guard gets here and locks the city down. Hell, the feds are just hoping that you put a ring on her hand so you can sign that contract and they have you by the balls."

The two-tone siren of Adams' radio sounded for three seconds, warning all airs of emergency traffic. Derrick checked his radio and saw that the battery had died while he slept. He turned on his car and car radio.

"Central dispatch to all airs, sixty-five-paul, code three. Thirty-seven Baker Street, cross with Shepherd's Lane.

Suspect: male, white, no shirt, holding people hostage in the coffee shop with a knife. Has already stabbed two customers. No further information. Any available negotiator, any available SWAT, switch to Central. Time is ten-eighteen."

Derrick had already popped his trunk for Adams to toss his bag in when the dispatcher said, *sixty-five-paul*. He stumbled out of the driver's seat and ran around to the passenger side to get dressed. His socks were stiff from the dried sweat of the day before.

Adams slammed the trunk closed, "Get in. I'll drive, you dress."

Derrick shoveled his pile of discarded uniform pieces and gun belt onto the floorboard and got in just as Adams put it in drive and sped out of the precinct parking lot.

He typed into the GPS the address. "Alright, Hart. You got eight minutes to get geared up or we are pulling up to the scene with you pulling up your pants looking like my cheap whore."

Derrick flung his soft body armor over his head and secured the Velcro straps across his chest. "Cheap or not, you still can't afford this."

"Fuck off, I make what you make!" Adams looked both ways at a red light as he worked the car sirens to different frequencies and sped through it.

"That's how I know you can't afford this ass," Derrick said.

It wasn't a fun experience, but Derrick had his uniform on a minute before arriving on scene. His gun belt was just off-center and his uniform pulled at an odd angle the way it was tucked in, but he'd have to make do.

The scene commander on the kidnapping situation was Sergeant Greer, whom Derrick was all too familiar with. Greer was a round, unpleasant man who was once Derrick's super-visor many years ago. Derrick knew the man was lazy and spiteful against anyone who aimed for anything above the minimum standard to keep their job. Fortunately, he wasn't Derrick's supervisor anymore, and he was not the scene commander anymore.

The SWAT sergeant, Bower, was already on the scene when Derrick and Adams arrived. Tom and Jeff had beaten them there by a few seconds, too. Adams was getting his rifle out of the trunk while Derrick quickly released his long gun from the rack between the seats. Chambering a round, he slung the rifle over his neck. He made the final adjustments to his hastily put on uniform while walking over to Tom and Jeff.

"Well, you look like shit," Tom said.

"I feel like it, too," Derrick replied.

"Hey guys!" Adams said, jogging behind Derrick.

Tom and Jeff exchanged an annoyed look they were infamous for. The coffee shop where the suspect and hostages were holed up was in the middle of a strip mall downtown. Patrol cars formed a horseshoe around the business and put up police tape twenty yards around the perimeter. The mob wasn't near what it was last night, but the roads were still clogged with thousands of civilians. It was like a rock concert had just been set loose on their crime scene.

"Greer says we don't got a negotiator working, so that's out," Sergeant Bower said as he joined his men. "The patrol officer working this zone has the suspect on the phone and is trying to Dr. Phil him to let the hostages out. I guess our suspect is either crazy or high out of his mind. I told Greer we'll give the officer ten more minutes to try and talk him down before we resolve this."

"How's the two stab victims?" Derrick asked, pulling his slung rifle behind his back. Patrol officers nearby were involved in a shouting match with a group of homeless trying to shove their way through the tape.

"Both stable for now from what I hear. Single stab wound in their stomachs," Bower replied.

"You all squared away? I know we all had eventful evenings last night. Especially you," Sergeant Bower said, smacking the folded map in his hand on Derrick's arm. "Downs sent me your use of force. You should have snuck a third shot on that asshole."

The group shared a snicker. Derrick should have known last night's bullshit had already made its way through the gossip channels of the department.

Cops are worse than a bunch of hens in a henhouse.

"Five by five," Derrick nodded, tucking in the rear of his uniform.

"This all that's coming?" Tom asked as he smoothed his bushy salt and pepper mustache down to his cheeks. He seemed on edge about something, or it could just be the lack of sleep. He was pushing forty, ten years older than Derrick.

Age catches up to you eventually.

"This is all we got," Sergeant Bower said.

"For real?" Adams said, wide-eyed. "What about Argento or Williams, or—"

"All gone," Bower shook his head. "Daniels, Smith, even that new girl, Perry, far as I can tell. They all 'no-call, no-showed.'"

Tom and Jeff exchanged a look and quickly averted their eyes.

"Damn..." Adams said what they all were thinking. The SWAT team was a lifestyle more than just a job. The handful of SWAT-certified operators worked together, trained together, went to the gym together, and went for drinks with one another ... it was a gut shot to think that they just up and left without even a word.

Of course, the phones and texting are so spotty nowadays, maybe they tried to reach out but couldn't.

"So I need affirmative answers from each of you on this: are you all good to deploy with just the five of us?" Bower folded his lean but muscular arms over his chest, eyeing his four men.

Jeff nodded silently, as was his way.

"Yeah, I'm here," Tom said, then winced at something like he had a pain in his side.

"Five by five," Derrick repeated with a sardonic smile.

"Hell yeah," Adams said, stretching his arms.

Bower smirked, "We need to get this kid some sleeping pills."

"Hey, you're not the one that has to ride with it," Derrick said, nodding toward the grinning Adams. Everyone had a laugh.

FOUR

DERRICK HART

The front of the store was all windows—large panes of glass so customers inside could drink coffee with the sun on their faces and passersby on the sidewalk could watch. This also gave the SWAT team no cover or concealment upon entry. Doing a brief reconnaissance from behind a patrol car with binoculars, Derrick could see an overturned table and broken glass scattered across the floor, probably where the assault began. The trail of blood droplets curved and led to a smear of blood across the wall near the front counter. Two victims suffering stab wounds had escaped with everyone else, but two customers and two waitresses were still unaccounted for.

First officers on the scene saw a shaggy-haired shirtless man shove a woman into the men's bathroom and made demands to 'speak to Jesus'. Needless to say, the patrol officer was not able to meet his demands.

Derrick fastened the chin strap of his ballistic helmet and moved with the rest of the team to the side of the front entrance. They made a stack of five along the side of the neighboring store in front of the first set of windows and prepped for entry.

"Ah, here we go! The killers have come!" A woman shouted from the gathered audience twenty yards back. "Look out inside! You're about to die!"

Derrick was at the front of the group, and he waited for the go order. It came in the form of a firm squeeze of his left triceps. He walked normally out from cover towards the front door. His eyes scanned from the front door to the windows, watching the interior for any signs of movement. Grabbing the door handle, he pulled it open and let his team file in. Their movements were quiet, steady, and smooth.

The last one in, Derrick picked the flow of travel each man moved to and could predict their planned sector of clearing. Tom and Jeff would clear the kitchen for additional threats. Sarge and the kid covered the short hall right behind the sitting section where the bathrooms were and where they believed the suspect and hostages were located. Derrick moved past them to the long hall that went to the back door and covered over it with his AR-15. When Tom and Jeff cleared the kitchen, they moved behind Derrick and squeezed his arm. He moved immediately. Derrick scanned the nooks and short corners all the way to the rear door and found nothing.

There were two doors in the back. A storage closet was empty except for brooms and cleaning supplies. The manager's office had one of the servers, a young black girl, curled under the computer desk. Derrick held a finger to his mouth when the girl started to cry. The girl caught the whimpers with her palms before they escaped her lips. Using his left hand, he quickly patted her down for weapons while Tom and Jeff covered the hallway.

As a team, they led the girl to the front door and handed her over to a patrolman, then returned to cover the bathrooms.

The patrol officer reported seeing them hide in the men's room, but there was a significant amount of time where no one watched the doors, so he could have moved to the women's. It was agreed upon before entry that Jeff, the senior man on the team, would lead the breach of the men's room with Tom and Adams, while Derrick and Bower would assault the women's room simultaneously.

The men stacked on their perspective walls and Tom and Adams readied their stun grenades. Sergeant Bower released his rifle and used his hands to open both doors. Pins were yanked and the stun grenades were chucked flawlessly into the two bathrooms.

The explosions echoed in the small tile bathrooms and sounded like a cannon had gone off. The fire alarm sounded, and Derrick made entry into the women's room. Rifle raised. His foot slid on blood and tripped over the girl's body, but he couldn't stop. He could feel Bower's breath on the back of his neck, urging him forward.

Screams erupted from an individual stall and Derrick saw furious movement in the handicap stall. Charging the handicapped stall, he booted the door open with such force it hit the wall and bounced back in Derrick's face as he entered.

More blood. Another body.

A shirtless man leaped on top of Derrick before he could reorient his rifle to address the threat. The distance was too close quarters for a long gun.

Derrick grabbed the man's wrist the second time he swiped a large bread knife at his face.

"He's come! He has come!" the man yelled in Derrick's face. A mix of snot and dirt pillowed in his unkempt mustache. Spittle from his lips rained across Derrick's clear faceplate.

Derrick was off-balance and leaning against the door as he struggled to keep the knife from inching any closer to his body.

A black blur whooshed across his face as the butt of Sergeant Bower's rifle smashed into the side of the suspect's face. The man dropped like a rock and Bower aimed his rifle down on him, ready to fire until he saw the knife fall from the suspect's grasp.

The rest of the team struggled to fit where all the action was happening. Adams, Jeff, and Tom huddled behind Sergeant Bower, wanting to help. Besides the dead hostage near the door, there was another covered in blood in the handicap stall. He was a young man with braces, and he wasn't moving.

The last hostage was in the other stall and was unharmed, but she screamed like she was. Adams exfill'ed her while Derrick and Bower dragged the unconscious suspect through one of his victim's blood and handcuffed him. Tom and Jeff got to work attempting first aid.

"All clear," Bower radioed into his mic. "Send in the medics. We've got more victims."

FIVE

DERRICK HART

The suspect writhed on the asphalt. The sticky blood that covered his loose, torn pants clung to the ground as he rocked from side to side, trying to turn back to look at his captor. Derrick gripped the suspect's biceps and stiff-armed him into the ground to keep him still.

"Relax," Derrick said. "If you calm down, I'll sit you up, but you've got to stop squirming."

"Let go! Get these off of me!" the suspect snarled through gnashing teeth.

That's all he was to Derrick now. *Suspect.* He didn't have time to learn their names anymore, or even their story beyond the essential parts of the crimes he'd committed. It wasn't like before when he would be called to a scene.

Felony warrant service. Barricaded suspect. The S.W.A.T. callout would last hours. Prep work, planning, coordinating, negotiations, execution of the plan, after-action report... But ever since the outbreak a few days ago, it didn't seem like Derrick or his team had time for anything other than completing the objective before another critical incident occurred.

It had been thirty-five hours since Derrick had been home to his house. He was sure Ginger, his black lab, had already pissed and shit all over the living room floor.

Twice, probably, he thought. *He never can hold it that long.*

It wasn't his fault.

Maybe I'll call Alyssa and see if she can...

"Jesus, is that all his blood?" the patrol officer asked as he stepped beside him.

Derrick glanced at the officer's name pin. *M. Jones.* He was a young man, early twenties, and new to the Birmingham Police Department. While Derrick was only twenty-nine years old, he had been with the department long enough to know most of the officers, even in a city this size.

"None of it's his," Derrick said, finally feeling the tenseness relax in the suspect's rigid body. Derrick turned the suspect to his side, then helped him to a seated position. "That's all his victims' blood."

Derrick pointed into the storefront of the coffee shop. Medics were just now leaving with their duffel bags and backpacks of equipment in hand. Per policy, they ran a strip on both victims' chests and confirmed there were no signs of life.

"You don't know that! You don't know that!" the suspect shouted at Derrick with crazed eyes and clacking teeth.

Thick gobs of a brown and black substance held his hair up in different directions like it was mousse. His arms would flex sporadically and pull at the flex cuffs that bound his wrists behind his back. The thick, zip-tie-looking restraints dug into his skin and left red cuts in his skin, but the suspect barely noticed the pain.

"Check again. Check em! They were part of it, man. You don't know. Check them. They were–were part of it. They were covering up the truth of the infection!"

"Okay, okay, we'll talk with you in a sec," Derrick spoke down to the suspect as he stood beside Officer Jones.

Derrick guessed there was some underlying mental illness mixed in with some meth coursing through his system, judging from how he acted. Derrick didn't think that excused him from murdering the two teenagers, but he was sure the courts would see it differently.

Even though the infection was still localized in Florida, the media coverage and horrific images on the internet from Miami had the entire country in an uproar. It was catnip for the paranoid and insane. Even the normal folks were creating their own conspiracy theories. The National Guard hadn't arrived in Birmingham yet, but they were due any day now.

Crazies were about to get crazier.

A glass storefront half a block down the road shattered and two patrol officers ran towards the culprits who still held rocks in their fists.

The National Guard was sorely needed.

Derrick sighed.

We need to wrap this up.

He heard dispatch radioing in his earpiece. It wasn't for him or SWAT this time, but soon enough another call would come, and they needed to be ready when it did.

Maybe I can grab a quick shower.

"Alright, you have your notepad handy?" Derrick asked.

Officer Jones tapped his breast pocket and took out his notepad and pen. "Yeah."

"That knife right there was in his hand when we made entry," Derrick said, pointing to the large bread knife with blood smeared across the side of it on the back of the officer's patrol car.

"This one right here," Derrick pointed to a black-handled steak knife beside it, "was in his back left pocket. I don't know if it was used in the homicides or not; it looks pretty clean."

"They're not dead!" the suspect blurted out. "They're just first!"

"After being taken into custody and being escorted out of the store," Derrick continued, ignoring the suspect's rants, "he stated freely and of his own volition, 'I didn't mean to kill them, but I had to.' You get that all?"

"Which one he tried to stab you with?"

"The big ass one."

Jones shook his head with a smirk. He finished scribbling his chicken scratch that only he could probably read. "Are you the one I'm subpoenaing for court?" the officer asked.

Derrick grimaced and looked up at the rest of his team, who was filing out of the store and back towards their vehicles. Each one of them looked more exhausted than the next. "Yeah, why not," Derrick muttered, and saw Officer Jones squinting at his nameplate. "Derrick Hart. Badge number 8242."

"Got it."

"You good with him?" Derrick asked, nodding towards the suspect.

"Yeah, you want to switch out cuffs?" Officer Jones asked.

Derrick looked down and saw his pair of flex cuffs stained with streaks of red and drying crimson blood from the victims inside. "Keep them, they're all yours."

"They were just first!" the suspect shouted as Derrick walked over to Sergeant Bower's SUV.

"Crazy son of a bitch," Sergeant Bower said as he tossed his ballistic helmet in the trunk and heaved his heavy armor vest over his head.

"Just a little bit, yeah," Derrick said, taking off his own helmet.

"You see those kids in there?" Bower shook his head. "The waitress was, what? Nineteen? Twenty years old, max?"

"It's only gonna get worse," Derrick sighed. The blacked-out SUV chirped its sirens twice as it slowly pulled away. "Is that Tom and Jeff? Where are they off to?"

"They are—"

"Hey, Sarge," Adams said, butting in between the two as he scratched his bald scalp. His ability to say the wrong thing at the wrong time rivaled only his cheerfulness, seemingly all the time. "We heading back to the station now? I'm freaking starving. I know it's messed up, but when we were escorting that dude outside, I kept staring at that turkey club sandwich on the table next to the door. I swear I almost swiped it, I'm so hungry."

"Uh yeah. I think so. At least until the next call," Bower said, looking over his shoulder to see if anyone else was near enough to overhear the new guy. "Hey, Adams, can you give Derrick and me a minute?"

"Heck yeah." Adams furrowed his brow and glanced at Derrick before quickly retreating to Derrick's charger.

Derrick moved closer to Bower with a confused look on his face.

"You know that vote?" Bower whispered, "That thing, the National Security Public Servant Act?"

"Yeah, what about it?"

"That vote's happening tonight or tomorrow. You know when the National Guard gets here? Tonight or tomorrow."

Derrick scrunched his brow, not following.

"It ain't a coincidence, Hart. The federal government gives our family a way out of the state, but only if cops agree to stay?

The National Guard are going to lock down the city. Us with everyone else."

Derrick nodded, having already guessed that. "Where did Tom and Jeff go?"

Bower sighed, reached into a side compartment of one of his gear bags, and removed two metal shields. They were Tom and Jeff's badges.

"They told me just now. I think they were too embarrassed to tell you," Bower said.

"They quit?" Derrick stared blankly as he digested the information. His gut reaction was betrayal. Even if in his head he understood what they were doing, Derrick couldn't help how he felt. He'd worked with Tom and Jeff for years now. They'd cleared hundreds of rooms together and put each other's lives in each other's hands just as many times.

"They're getting their families out of the city before it's too late," Bower looked over his shoulder. "You need to think of doing the same. Single guys like you and Adams get used and abused twice as much as the rest of us because you ain't got no one at home bitching at you to stop working so much."

Tom and Jeff had what Derrick didn't.

Wives... children... family.

"What'd you say to them? Tom and Jeff, when they left?"

"I said," Bower took a deep breath. "I said I understood. I said I probably wouldn't be far behind them."

Shock broke across Derrick's eyes as he shot a look at his sergeant. A mix of surprise and disbelief shaded his expression. Bower grimaced at his friend.

"Sooner or later, you have to ask yourself with this job, how much are you willing to give for this city, you know? You can't save them all ..."

Sergeant Bower had been one of Derrick's closest friends in

the department. Having not grown up with a father, Derrick had looked up to Bower as a mentor and, as silly as it sounded, a father figure for years. On their weekends off, Derrick and his team would do grill-outs at the Sarge's house or go on the occasional fishing trip to Cosby Lake, where they'd spend the day draining beers.

Derrick looked at Bower as a guide, not just in this department, but in life.

And Bower is leaving. Does that mean I should go?

Bower had a beautiful wife and kids who were all nearly teenagers. Derrick knew *the job* was a bigger part of his life than Bower's or his other teammates'. The closest thing he had to a family in Birmingham was Alyssa, and things were ... complicated with her.

Derrick nodded and finally spoke, "You know, on the day I was pinned, you told me SWAT is a calling and not a job."

Bower looked away from Derrick, pursing his lips.

"That it meant you were the last line of defense for the entire city ..." Derrick continued. "That SWAT meant that you were willing to go farther, and dig deeper, and go places that others can't—or won't—go in order to save lives."

"Yeah, I know," Bower sighed.

"Hart! Sarge! Turn up your radios," Adams hollered back at them. "We got a good one."

They both fumbled with their radios on their belts. Twisting the volume knob, Derrick heard dispatch's grating voice in his ear. "Any available units switch to South-East, Code 8000. Shots fired, shots fired..."

Derrick looked back at Adams, who hung out of the passenger seat of his Charger like a basset hound waiting for his owner to take him to the park. Derrick handed the two silver badges back to Bower.

"So, are *we* going?" he asked. The words seemed to carry more weight than he'd intended.

Bower thumbed the badges, staring at them for a long minute as he thought, then nodded. "Yeah. Let's go."

SIX

AARON VANDERKAMP

Morning had come and gone. Afternoon had come and was on its way out. The boy's body remained. Aaron tried to avoid looking at it as much as possible. He didn't go into the kitchen at all, not even when he was thirsty. It was for the best; they needed to conserve their water. The electricity came on around ten in the morning and lasted only a few hours. They had filled the bathtub and a few buckets with water and charged all their electronics, but the power had been off for the rest of the day. If this outage was planned, his parents didn't know about it.

Brad didn't seem to have a problem looking at the dead body that, by now, was decomposing on the back lawn. He and Michael made jokes and stared at it for so long their mother had to yell at them both to stop looking at it. Aaron was concerned for his mother. Ever since hanging up with the police dispatchers, she had locked herself in her bedroom, whispering prayers on her knees. Their family wasn't the most religious. They went to church every Sunday, mainly to appease his mom. She thought if she prayed hard enough she could save her sons' souls ... and her husband's.

Aaron didn't think it worked like that.

They were on hold with 911 for sixty-eight minutes before an impatient woman answered with an emotionless, "What's your emergency?"

The trespasser's body was cold by then and the panic of the emergency had left everyone's voice. Aaron was just happy to hear that someone eventually answered. Around the forty-five-minute mark, Brad half-joked that maybe there were no more police or government. Maybe the zombie apocalypse really had begun. He wore a half-grin that disturbed Aaron, like his brother didn't fully appreciate what had just happened in their backyard.

After their father fumed at the dispatcher for a minute over how long he had to wait to get through, and the dispatcher threatened to hang up on him if he didn't stop cursing at her, then Michael took the phone and explained the situation.

Calmness was in the dispatcher's voice as she asked follow-up questions like, *Is anyone hurt? Is the suspect still alive? Are there any more suspects?*

Michael, sharing his father's temper, did a remarkable job of keeping his spiteful comments to himself. The conversation ended with the dispatcher stating with a sigh, "We'll get someone out there as soon as we can."

As soon as you can? Someone was shot—killed...

It took another five hours before a single patrol officer arrived, coming to the door with his notepad and pen out like they were reporting a stolen bicycle. He walked around the property and inspected the body. Aaron overheard him say into his radio, "Obvious signs of death."

After twenty minutes of talking to each family member individually, photographing the scene with his cell phone, and inspecting the weapons, the officer delivered a small pamphlet with his name and report number on it.

"Someone will come along to collect the body shortly," the officer said as he was halfway out the door.

Aaron sat on the purple ottoman, looking out the living room window, and watched the sunset. There weren't any pretty colors that sometimes lit up the sky. The light gray over-cast sky only darkened to a gray-black, and a shadow seemed to hover over the street. And the corpse remained in their backyard.

Michael patrolled the interior and exterior of the house throughout the day. Aaron didn't think anyone had asked him to, but he'd taken it upon himself, strolling with slow, purposeful steps in circles with his rifle held casually in his arms. He had two more magazines for his rifle shoved into the butt pocket of his jeans, and a flashlight sticking out of his front pocket.

"Hey Mike..." Aaron started, but he regretted it imme-diately.

Michael stopped in front of the window. Aaron shot a look towards the hallway. Mom and Dad had been in their bedroom for some time, arguing in hushed tones like they usually did, as if their kids couldn't hear. Brad had been reading comics in his bedroom ever since Mom scolded him for staring at the body.

"What's up?" Michael narrowed his eyes, recognizing the beginnings of a rare serious conversation between brothers.

"I just..." Aaron double-checked that their parents' door was closed. "Isn't this a little weird? Leaving the body back there?"

Michael shrugged. "Cops said not to touch it. They'll come eventually."

Aaron nodded. "He said... the guy was unarmed."

Michael's eyebrows raised half an inch, "So?"

"I don't... it just feels weird. Do you think he should have?"

"Shot him? Fuck yeah," Michael sat beside his brother and

rested his rifle on the seat beside him. "Dude, there were three of them. One of the others could have taken his gun. What if they got inside? What if they had knives or they called the other shit bags from the street in? What are we going to do? Call the cops?"

Aaron nodded. He didn't enjoy thinking about things like that. Of how bad things could have gone.

"It just feels weird. Everything, you know?"

"World's changing, bro. It ain't going to be all hack and slash like Brad is beaten' off to, but it could be close. If we want to survive, we've got to adapt." Michael grabbed the barrel of his rifle and brought the weapon between his knees, shaking it as if Aaron didn't see it. "You need to get ready. You might need to do the same soon."

Aaron looked at the couch end table over his shoulder where his father's pistol sat. *My pistol.* He hadn't touched it since the dead boy's friends had fled.

"Hey, just remember, it's them or it's you. It's as simple as that," Michael shouldered Aaron. "Last night it was that dude or Dad, and Dad fuckin' won."

Aaron looked at his eldest brother and saw the corner of a cheerful smile on his face. For the first time, he understood what all their extended family and parents' friends used to always say:

Aaron is his mother's son.

Of course, he was his mother's son and so were his brothers, but that wasn't what they were saying. Aaron took after his mother, unlike his two elder brothers. Aaron was a better wrestler, but he didn't like to compete. He enjoyed spending time with his father, but he didn't want to go hunting with him. It was strange, but as close as he was to Michael now, looking up at his reassuring smile, Aaron had never felt further apart.

"...my responsibility to take care of this family and it's my decision!" his father's voice went from muffled to booming as he opened the bedroom door and stormed into the living room carrying a large luggage bag. He surveyed his two sons on the ottoman and yelled for the third to join them. Brad jogged into the living room like it was Christmas morning, with his rifle clutched in his hand.

"Don't run with that thing," his mother warned. She remained in the entryway with her arms folded, as far away from their father as possible in silent protest.

"Sons," their father started, "you're going to take the night and pack what you need and only what you need. One suitcase each."

"Why? Where are we going?" Aaron asked.

"Your grandma's cabin up near Florence. We'll pack up food and water for the drive and—"

"Ugh, Dad..." Brad complained. He hated the annual summer trips to the cabin. It barely had electricity, didn't have a TV, and he couldn't play his video games, which he obsessed over. "But they don't have the internet there. They don't even have the news. How are we going to know what's going on?"

"Genius," Michael said, "we don't have those things right now either."

"Can I at least bring my TV and Xbox—" Brad said, but he was silenced by his father.

"No! Clothes, photos, phones, laptops, money, food, and water. That's it. Things that can't be replaced. We leave first thing in the morning."

Aaron looked into the kitchen. "What about the body?"

His mother covered her eyes, shaking her head.

"If the police don't want to do their fucking job, then so be it!" his father snapped.

The quiet tension returned to the room—the feeling of stepping between their parents' argument and having nowhere to escape. Aaron only stared out the window at the darkening night, waiting for the moment to pass.

After a moment, it was Michael who shoved the conversation onward. "Uh, Dad, we don't got much food left. Some canned foods, mostly soups, and condiments. Maybe some macaroni and cheese."

"It's expired," Brad said.

Their dad wiped away a layer of sweat on his brow as he paced a circle near the front door. It was hot today. With no AC and no breeze, the house had felt like an oven set to low all day. Aaron thought he could smell the body's rot.

"Okay," his father finally said. "Okay, we'll stop by one of those food ration zones they had on the news this morning. I think they turned the Grocery Superstore into one."

"Those lines were huge," Brad said.

Father held up a hand to Brad, clearly getting annoyed with his complaints since he learned he was leaving his gaming console behind. "We'll go on the way to the cabin, all of us. We'll leave early—four in the morning. We'll get there before the line forms and be on the road by late morning, okay?"

The five of them exchanged looks of insecurity. Mom still wore her scowl, a remnant of their argument before.

"Look, I know this is scary, but I need you three to be men about this. This is dangerous. Your mother says her Bible calls this the end of time. That's fine..."

Their mother scoffed at his remarks and returned to the bedroom. The door slamming was her response.

"I call it the end of democracy," Father continued. "We been getting soft as a country for some time, and now the chickens have come home to roost. You understand? So no complaining. Do as you're told and follow my lead until we get to that cabin."

"Yes, sir," the three boys replied.

SEVEN

JOHN MILES

Miles sat at his kitchen table. His gun belt dug into his right hip where it normally did. He'd been wearing the police uniform for almost a year now, and still his body hadn't gotten used to it. Bethany always inspected his thighs and hips when they were in bed together. Black bruises populated his left thigh, where his magazine pouch dug when he sat. Red and brown streaks of damage to his skin were left behind where the lip of his holster sawed into his side when he walked. There were a few others, but none were crippling, just annoying. He'd thought by now his body would be used to the job.

It was strange sitting in his apartment in full uniform. He felt out of place, like wearing a tuxedo at McDonald's. Usually, when he went to work and returned, he didn't linger in his uniform too long. The kids, somehow or another, always made him almost late every day, so he had to hurry out the door. When he returned after a shift of arresting homeless people covered in lice or working bloody murder scenes, he didn't want the girls hugging him when he came home. Not after the places he had been and the scenes he'd worked.

He heard Bethany put on a movie for the girls in their bedroom. It was a two-bedroom, eight-hundred-square-foot apartment with a married couple and twin four-year-old girls living in it. Miles could stand in the front doorway and hear his kids' conversation in the back bedroom. There were no secrets in his home.

Miles took another sip of his coffee and flipped the packet of papers before him to the back page. There was a gaping hole in the back of his throat that fell to a widening chasm in his belly. He was scared, and he didn't like it. He couldn't let Bethany see. Grimacing, he scribbled his signature on the back two pages and closed the packet of papers when he heard her force the ill-fitted kids' bedroom door shut. It never latched. The friction of the warped wood of the door held it shut.

Bethany entered the kitchen and squeezed her husband's shoulder. She opened a cupboard to get a coffee mug out, but then saw that Miles had already poured her a cup when he was filling his 'Back the Blue' travel mug for work. She smiled appreciatively, though her eyes were still full of sorrow.

"Is that it?" Bethany asked, nodding to the packet in front of him.

Her soft, delicate features had been stricken from the stress of long days and sleepless nights. She might not have been wearing riot gear and working the riots like Miles had, but the life of a cop's wife was a different kind of service. Gray-shadowed bags had formed under his wife's eyes. The nails of her thumb and forefinger were chewed into the pink, a nervous tick she had brought with her from childhood. A few years ago, Miles and Bethany were high school sweethearts at their senior prom. They were kids themselves, just starting their lives together. Now he had just signed a 'suicide contract', and this might be the last time he'd see his wife. He fought to keep the frown from showing on his face.

Miles nodded and took a drink of his coffee, not trusting his voice not to falter. He knew the government wanted him to sign badly, because, in a rare move of organization for the federal government, they had the Honor Bound contract templates available to download before the bill had even passed.

Bethany released an exasperated sigh and shrunk a little into the chipped and wobbly hotel liquidation table they sat at. "I just don't understand. How can they make you sign that? How can they force you to stay?"

"They don't have to. You saw it on the news, interstates were backed up in every direction. People are starting to try to walk to a different state. They don't need the National Guard to block all the roads and trap us here; people have done it on their own."

"Well, how will getting out of here be any better for us if you sign that thing?" Bethany sneered when she nodded at the papers like they were a squashed spider between them.

"I'm not sure. Helicopters? Planes?" Miles shrugged, leaning back in his chair and hearing the old wood groan.

"They grounded all flights days ago," she said.

"If they pass this Honor Bound bill tonight or tomorrow morning, the bill clearly states that if a person in an essential job, like law enforcement, signs the contract, up to four of his immediate family members will be transported to a touching state of their choosing." Miles rubbed his forehead with the palm of his hand, then gestured at the papers angrily. "I don't know how they'll do it, but if they want me to stay here and police, then they'll find a way to get you to Tennessee."

"Okay," Bethany mumbled weakly.

Miles winced, and his eyes went wide as he reached across the table to grab her hand. "No, honey, I'm sorry. I wasn't mad at—"

"I know," Bethany replied with an understanding expression. Her hand grasped his, and he felt the hole inside him grow.

He bit his lower lip hard, until the pain brought his mind away from his desire to cry. His wife must've seen more than he wanted her to, because she squeezed his hand tighter, and her whispered voice became more desperate.

"Maybe you don't sign them," she said with wide, wet eyes. "Maybe we just go. We go now. Maybe the roads won't be as bad if we go west to Mississippi."

Miles squeezed his wife's hand back and for a moment, allowing his mind to chase the fantasy she had crafted. Loading up the kids in his police car and using his blue lights and sirens to get as far west as they could. It was the memory of the news and the video that showed a family with small children walking along the side of the road in the scorching sun that soured the fantasy for him.

Scooting the chair away from the table, he let go of his wife. Miles looked down to gather his thoughts. "Um, I signed the papers already. You just need to sign them."

In his peripheral vision, he saw Bethany recoil at his words. He tapped at both of his breast pockets, then removed a stack of plastic swipe cards from his left pocket. At the bottom of the stack was the card he wanted, and he placed it on the manilla folder beside the Honor Bound contract. "This is my commission card, my APOSTC certification, and our marriage license. If the bill passes and I'm not back from my shift, I want you to just go. Just take the kids and go, okay?"

When Miles stood, his wife launched into his arms. Her face was buried in his chest as she cried, but he couldn't feel her tears. The body armor he wore beneath his uniform kept them out. He kissed the top of her head as he held her tight and savored her smell. The natural scent of her hair conditioner mixed with the coconut of her lotion. Miles tried to memorize the aroma, but felt like he forgot it the moment he pulled away.

Grabbing his work bag and shotgun he had resting against the kitchen sink, he looked at his watch. He was going to be late for the start of the third shift.

"Are—are you going to say goodbye to the girls?" Bethany blurted out in desperation. She had seen him kiss the girls good-night before she put on a movie for them, but Miles knew what she meant.

She wants me to say goodbye to the girls in case they never see me again.

A knot of sadness lurched in his throat, and he did every-thing he could to keep from crying.

"No." Miles cleared his throat. "I already did."

They hugged and kissed one final time before Miles carried his things downstairs to the parking lot. The entire way, he was haunted by the feeling that he had forgotten something. Left something behind.

My family.

Miles neared his patrol car parked in its usual spot at the back of the lot and saw a spiderweb of cracked glass spiraling out from an impact mark on the back window. The softball-sized rock likely used sat in the middle of the parking lot, not far from his vehicle. At the front windshield, a single piece of paper was tucked under his windshield wipers.

'FUK U PIG'

The words were written above a crude drawing of a stick figure and a pig that made him snicker as the drawing and writing were worse than what his daughters were capable of.

Crinkling the paper into a ball of trash, there was an imperceptible shift that occurred in Miles. His back stiffened, his shoulders rolled back, and his eyes scanned his surroundings purposefully. Suddenly, the uniform didn't feel so unnatural on him.

EIGHT

DERRICK HART

Derrick pulled the car to the side of the street. He was around the block from her apartment complex, which he thought made it less creepy, though he didn't know why. Fewer people were loitering in the street in Alyssa's part of town. He could tell the riots hadn't touched this area yet. It was nearly eleven o'clock at night. If the past nights were any indicator for tonight, the crowd would start to get rowdy downtown right now.

Pulling out his phone, he spent another ten minutes staring at it, mentally tossing all the reasons he shouldn't make the call before ultimately tapping Alyssa's number on the screen.

Of course, cellular connections were so bad he had to hang up and redial her number fourteen times before the call was finally connected.

"Derrick?" Alyssa answered. Her voice was as much a mixture of surprise as intrigue.

A smile broke across his face before he could stop it. "Hey, 'Lys."

"Oh my god, I've been worried about you. I've been

watching the news like all day. The protests have been crazy! Have you had to work any of them?"

Derrick ran his thumb and forefinger over his eyelids, pinching the bridge of his nose. "Yeah, I've worked some of them."

"That's crazy. I bet that was pretty fun," she said.

Derrick could tell she was sniffing for details. She had always loved getting the inside track on all the crashes and murders that happened in the city when they dated. It gave her something to *dish* about at work.

"Hey, can we talk?"

"Um, yeah, sure," Alyssa said. Her tone turned somber. There was a brief pause that quickly turned awkward. "What's up?"

"Uh, I meant in person, if that's—"

"Oh," Alyssa sounded less sure of herself now. "I can't. Not right now. There's no power to my block. The stupid magnetic lock to the parking lot gates won't open."

Derrick thought of how to say what he needed to say without sounding creepy but decided there wasn't a way. "I'm here. I'm down the road from your apartment complex," he blurted out.

"Oh, okay. I'll... I'll be right down," she said.

"Okay," he said and hung up.

Derrick parked his Charger on the street and locked the doors. He left the windows cracked to air it out. After another full day of heat and running call-to-call, his undercover police car was beginning to smell like a frat house.

He had managed to get home for a couple of hours. He let Ginger outside and watched him do a dozen laps of sprints in the backyard while Derrick cleaned up the messes he'd left behind in the living room. Derrick wanted to do a load of laundry, but the blackout was in his section of town. Instead, he used up what remained of the water in the pipe to refill Ginger's water bowl and taking a rudimentary shower/bath before the shower stopped working. Ginger enjoyed the brief nap that Derrick and he shared. It would have been tough to sleep if they'd known it was the last time they would nap together.

Forty-Eight Street West Apartments where Alyssa lived were some of the better apartments in the city. They had a gated parking lot, twelve-foot fencing, and security cameras that covered the points of entry into the ten-story building.

She should be safe here. For a time.

The sound of a heavy metal door unlatching captured Derrick's attention. He approached the gate and tried to use the doorknob. *Locked.* The magnetic swipe pad for a key card sat as dark as the night sky. Alyssa approached, her flip-flops tapping the pavement with every step. She was wearing baggy black pajama bottoms and an oversized hoodie. *His* hoodie, in fact. Her hair was pulled back in a ponytail and her face was washed of makeup, which told Derrick she was either in bed when he called or was about to be in bed.

"Hey," she said, wearing a polite smile.

"Hey," he replied.

The two were stiff and uncomfortable seeing each other. They hadn't seen each other in almost a month. Not since returning from a trip to Pigeon Forge, and she'd told him she wanted to go on a break.

"You on duty?" Alyssa's eyes flicked down to his uniform.

"About to be. I'm headed in."

"I thought you worked day-shift now?"

"Uh, everyone kinda works always right now," he said with a shrug. "How about you? How's work been?"

Alyssa rolled her eyes and sighed. "A nightmare. I never knew things could be slow and fucking insane at the same time.

I had like three events scheduled for this week that I had to scramble to delay and get in touch with vendors. Then I have five more scheduled for next week, including a wedding that the bride doesn't want to cancel just in case this all 'blows over' by then."

Derrick laughed at that. The thought of a bride arguing with her wedding planner about cataclysmic world events affecting her *special day* was amusing to imagine.

"Did you tell her you didn't think the apocalypse will be wrapped up in time for her to walk down the aisle?"

"In so many words," Alyssa smiled. "Let's just say I don't think she's leaving me a five-star review online."

While Alyssa spoke, the stiffness of her body loosened and she neared the gate Derrick was leaning his hands on. He had noticed it before, of course. Alyssa loved talking about her business and various projects or trips she was in the middle of planning. They changed her, brought her to life. Just talking about work awoke her personality like a rising sun.

"You don't mean that, do you?" she asked.

"What?"

"You don't think this is really the apocalypse or anything?" Alyssa's eyes narrowed. She, like everyone else, suspected that the police knew details that the rest didn't. The sad truth was the cops were as blind as everyone else. They just lived what everyone else watched on the nightly news.

"No," Derrick replied reflexively.

"Derrick?"

His heart beat half a beat quicker at the sound of his name on her lips. He shook away the spell it cast upon him.

"I don't know. Probably not, but..."

"But what?"

"But a lot of cops are starting to quit, you know? Take their families and try to make a run for it."

"I know. Before the power went out, I was watching the news about that bill. The National Security whatever. It's nuts! It's basically the draft being reinstated. I can't believe the president is getting away with it! You know, a lot of people think the government is behind all this," Alyssa took a deep breath as she continued to talk.

Derrick smiled. He missed just listening to her talk; it relaxed him.

"But people here are quitting? Anyone I know?" Alyssa asked.

"I heard Moore left, Erickson. Tom and Jeff left today," he said.

"Jeff? Really? He was so close to retirement though."

"Bower was going to leave today, I think. I think I kinda guilted him into staying," Derrick shook his head, allowing his thoughts to consume him. "I don't know, he still might go tomorrow."

"What about you?" Alyssa asked. She was close to the gate now. Her hands grabbed the metal bars that separated them like a prisoner would.

"No, I, uh, I thought about trying to get to Brandon up in Nashville, but last I spoke to him, he was thinking about re-upping, signing the Honor Bound contract to get back into the Army."

Alyssa rolled her eyes, "That fucking moron *would* be the guy who'd sign up for this shit."

Derrick laughed. He always enjoyed the love-hate relationship his best friend and Alyssa had. For a moment, Derrick caught Alyssa's eyes, and he thought of all the things he wanted to say but stopped himself. Then he remembered what he needed to say.

"Yeah, no, um," Derrick started. He looked down so he would not be distracted. "I wanted to talk because I don't think

I'm going anywhere ... So I thought if I'm not leaving anyways, and they pass that bill ... maybe I'll sign one of those contracts, too."

Alyssa screwed up her face and shook her head, "But why would you sign it? I heard it only helps if you have a..."

A murky understanding grew in her eyes and Derrick watched her hands release the bars as she leaned away from the gate an inch.

There it is, Derrick thought as he felt the familiar sting in his chest just as he saw the worry on her face.

"Look, I know you said no before and thought I sprung it on you out of nowhere, or whatever, but this isn't that. I know we're ... on break or whatever," he said, "but I'm just letting you know that since I'm staying here already, I'd sign the contract for you if we got married."

The pause before she spoke was almost as long as the one after the first time he'd asked for her hand in marriage. "Derrick, I'm not asking you to do this. I'd never ask—"

"I know, I know," Derrick raised a hand in understanding. "That's why I'm here offering it. The infection is spreading in Florida, and it could get bad here. I just thought it might be safer for you in Tennessee. You could go stay with Karen and Brandon."

"And I still haven't decided if marriage is a right fit for me," Alyssa's eyes changed to an apology; like she was saying no all over again.

Derrick smiled, taking a step back from the gate. "This isn't a trick, 'Lys. I'm not trying to secretly throw a net over you so you can't escape." Alyssa snickered and rolled her eyes. Derrick relaxed his posture a bit. "If we did this, we can have it annulled in a few months after this all blows over."

"I appreciate it," Alyssa said, her eyes searching for his. "You've been amazing to me considering everything I've put you through these last weeks. I'm sorry I... I don't know, I'm just sorry."

Derrick nodded and checked his watch. "I've got to go, but you can think about it, okay?"

"Thanks," Alyssa said.

Derrick turned to leave and made it a few paces away before Alyssa called for him.

"Be careful," Alyssa yelled to him, and Derrick smiled back.

NINE

AARON VANDERKAMP

Dawn was breaking, and the Vanderkamp family had been standing in line for three hours. It hadn't moved in the first two and a half hours because the grocery superstore hadn't opened until now. Apparently, over a hundred and fifty other people had the same idea as Aaron's father, as the line had already circled the enormous parking lot by the time they arrived. Aaron only counted up to one-fifty. There were more than that.

Police patrolled the line like prison guards at a chow hall. Their faces were sunken and humorless, their eyes dark and tired. Aaron was sweating bullets when they first got in line, despite the cool breeze that night. Their dad demanded they each carry their weapons with them everywhere. Aaron's brothers and father each carried a duffel bag that stored their rifles. Aaron had his pistol zipped in the front pocket of his backpack he wore. Every time one of the cops paced by his section of the line, Aaron swore the officer's investigative eyes could see right through the fabric of his backpack. He touched the pocket zippers at least a dozen times an hour to make sure they were still closed.

How do people in the movies just slide guns into their waistbands? Aren't they afraid the gun will just fall out?

At one point, when the sun shot its first rays of yellow across the sky, a young officer who had been there since before they first arrived singled Aaron out. Even now, Aaron wasn't sure if the officer was just being nice or had some ulterior motive.

"Hey, how you doing today?" he asked, giving Aaron's shoulder a light tap to get his attention.

As soon as Aaron's eyes leveled with the silver badge on the man's chest, his heart beat faster and faster in his chest.

"Good, s—sir. I mean, I'm good."

"That's good. I'm glad we've got a nice breeze tonight, I'm liking that. I'm Officer Miles. What's your name?"

The weight of the handgun felt like it tripled in his backpack. Aaron swallowed and started to speak. He only got out a syllable of his name before his father's paw fell onto his shoulder.

"Uh, this is my son," he said as he stepped in front of Aaron. "You got a problem?"

"No, uh, no problem, sir, just making small-talk. Been a long night; just trying to stay awake," Officer Miles smiled.

"Then you ain't got a reason to talk to him," his father said.

The bright eyes and innocent smile Aaron once saw on the officer disappeared like a magic trick, leaving a practiced blank expression that seemed to look through his father rather than at him.

"Yes, sir," the officer said. He stepped away without looking at Aaron, then his father did the same.

His Dad's overbearing protectiveness annoyed Aaron, but left him puzzled for the next few hours as to why his father had reacted that way and what the officer could have gained from asking his name.

Mom was the only one without a weapon. She refused on principle to take the other, smaller handgun Dad had. She was going to wait in the car until they got closer to the front of the line, but when they realized they had to park a mile and a half away, Father decided it was best if they all stuck together.

The line was moving now. Not much; a step every couple of minutes. It felt more substantial than it looked, but after standing in one place for hours, they welcomed any progress. No one seemed to know how it worked. Aaron squinted and could see people going into the first vestibule for a moment, then leave with a bag or two of something. They weren't letting people into the store to shop like a normal grocery store, and his father was getting angry about it.

"Fucking government," he grumbled under his breath as he began to pace in place.

"John!" Mom whispered, shooting a look at Aaron.

Aaron made a show of rolling his eyes and shaking his head. He hated that they still treated him like a child even though he was fifteen. He and his older brother, Brad, looked so alike people thought they were twins. Was this going to happen for the rest of his life? Would Aaron be thirty-four years old and Mom still would play the earmuff game with him anytime someone cursed.

"I don't see anyone getting much food, Dad," Michael said, staring across the parking lot at the entrance.

"If it even is food. They could be giving them mouthwash for all we know," Brad said.

Father was still cursing to himself. "Can't keep their hands off private companies or their damn citizens." He kicked a small stone hard into the center of the parking lot. It rolled between two officers and gained the attention of the surrounding people in the line as well as the curiosity of the officers.

"John, people are looking," mother whispered.

His dad had stopped at an ATM to top off the cash he had at the house. The plan was to fill every available space in their minivan with food, water, batteries, and toiletries before hitting the road. That didn't look like a possibility anymore.

"Even if they're getting food, it's only one or two meals it looks like," Michael said. "We really going to wait in this giant line for a couple meals, Dad?"

Mother stuck her head in the middle of her children and spoke in a hushed tone, "Maybe that's all they can afford. Maybe when we get up there, we can give them a list or something and they'll go get what we want. John, do you have a pen and paper? We should've made a grocery list before coming."

TEN

JOHN MILES

"Are you going to do something?!"

"We've been out here all night!"

"It's almost noon!"

"This ain't legal; this a private establishment. Government can't keep us out like this."

Miles paced back and forth along the endless line of people that stretched across the asphalt parking lot. His presence—no, really his uniform and the uniform of the six other police officers—was the only deterrent that kept this teetering house of cards from collapsing.

"Fuck you, pig!" a man shouted from Miles' backside.

Miles turned with a flare of anger inside him and thought about the smashed window on his police car. He knew he should ignore the insults. Laugh them off, the senior officers on his detail had said.

Occupational hazard, they'd say. *Comes with the job. You'll get used to it.*

Miles' eyes found the man with the loud mouth. He was a bald man with a t-shirt two sizes too large and sweat stains around the neck and pits. The man's eyes looked like everyone else's. Exhausted. Angry. Scared. They looked like Miles' eyes. He knew it was a coincidence. The man here who called him a pig wasn't the same guy who'd smashed his patrol car window at his apartment complex. But Miles was running on fumes. He'd been on his feet patrolling this line for fourteen hours now with no end in sight.

"What, bitch?" the bald man balked. "Yeah, you heard me. Fuck you! What you going to do?" the bald man tugged at his shirt, which stuck to his sweaty gut as he stepped forward out of the line.

"Sir, get back in line," Miles said, quieter than he'd intended.

"Or what? Yeah, you a rookie cop, ain't ya? I can see it. You just a rookie," the man became more brazen as he neared Miles. More disgruntled voices shouted support to the troublemaker. Everyone was so fed up that anyone who balked at the rules was considered a hero.

Miles cleared his throat and tried again, "Sir, get back in line now or—or you'll have to leave."

"Fuck you, I'm going inside," the man said as he walked towards Miles. Behind Miles was another hundred yards of parking lot with zigzagging lines of people waiting to get inside the Grocery Superstore. Miles' cheeks went red and his eyes blank as his mind maneuvered past the exhaustion clogging his thoughts for a solution.

Is this an arrestable offense? Do I go hands-on? I don't have any backup nearby. If I do and he fights me this could turn bad if the others in the crowd join him. Should I just let him walk by to keep the peace? But if others see him cut ahead, won't everyone charge the front?

Miles recalled the Lieutenant's words from last night's roll call. "We barely have enough officers to staff this place and we don't have arrest teams. Don't make any arrests unless you clear it through a Sergeant first. We don't have the manpower to spare."

Miles' hands shook as the lumbering man stomped towards him. Miles threw his palms up to stop him, but even Miles saw there was no confidence in his attempt.

"Sir," Miles said.

"Hey! What are you doing? Get back, you!" a familiar voice hollered over Miles' shoulder. "Yeah, *you*, stop right there! You take another step and you're goin' with me!"

"Man, I'm not doing shit!" the bald man cursed and threw his hands up but didn't advance any farther.

Officer Randle stormed in front of Miles. He stabbed his finger back in the line's direction. "Get back in the line now or I will drag you off this property."

It was strange. Randle had come out of the same academy class as Miles, but they were two completely separate officers. Miles was more athletic and even had a couple of inches in height on Randle, but Randle had something else that Miles searched for in himself. It was like he was more rugged and wise to the streets or something. Miles rolled his eyes as he was now following and backing Randle up.

"Come on, I just need groceries and you guys out here only letting a few in at a time. I been out here all day!" The bald man complained.

"Alright, let's go. Come on," Randle said as he stepped to the bald man's side and reached for his arm. "You think I'm playing?"

"Okay, okay! Damn, man," the bald man retreated backward. His hands swiped at the air in frustration as Randle followed him back to the line. "Fuckin' Nazis, Goddamn."

Once Randle had seen the man get back in line and the rest of the onlookers had seen what would happen if they got out of the line, Randle returned to Miles with a nod. When he was close enough to talk so the civilians couldn't hear, Miles said, "Thanks for that."

"No problem," Randle replied, rolling his eyes. "Shit's getting nutty out here, isn't it?"

"National Guard can't get here soon enough," Miles said.

Randle chewed his lip as he looked back at his section of the line to make sure they stayed put. "I don't know if I'm looking forward to the Army coming or not. You hear they passed that suicide contract bill?"

"They did?" Miles sounded surprised, but he didn't know why. He knew it would pass. It was the equivalent of the Patriot Act after 9/11. The bill was loaded with funding and emergency powers, all the political pundits predicted it would pass with a unanimous vote.

"Yeah, like four or five hours ago," Randle said. "Sarge heard it on the news inside. You gonna sign yours?"

Miles heard the words, but he didn't respond. His mind searched for where his wife and daughters were.

Four or five hours ago? Had they already left the house? Were they already being loaded into planes or buses to go to Tennessee?

Gunfire elevated Miles' heart rate before he even had time to process what was going on. It was loud enough that he knew the shooting was coming from the parking lot, but it wasn't in the immediate vicinity. Randle drew his pistol as Miles reached for his radio, but other voices were already keyed up on the mic.

"Shots fired, shots fired!" a female officer's voice crackled through the mic as the lines of people began to scatter and scream.

"Over here, come on!" Randle yelled back to Miles as they ran between a wall of people who sprinted for the store. Miles pulled his Glock 17 handgun from his holster and could feel how sweaty his palm was as he squeezed the grip. Farther down the parking lot near the road he heard engines roar.

"Get back! Get—they're charging inside! They're overrunning the supermarket!" Miles' radio squawked.

Two pickup trucks mounted a curb and rammed the metal four-foot barrier that surrounded the large parking lot. Men and women at the back of the line sprinted to keep out of the way of the front bumper. More cars that had waited in line along the street for hours to get in followed suit and bottomed out as they sped over top of the curb.

"Hey!" Randle shouted. "Drop the gun! Drop the—"

Miles turned to see who Randle was giving commands to, but the crowd was too thick. A burst of gunfire exploded as Randle engaged a suspect and bullets littered the crowd. An older woman and two men beside her screamed when they were shot by stray bullets, and they fell down in front of Miles.

Miles froze, half wanting to bend down to help the wounded and half still looking for the shooter and his friend. The break in the crowd allowed him to see Randle for a moment.

He was laying face-down on the asphalt.

ELEVEN

AARON VANDERKAMP

Aaron didn't remember how he got to the ground, but he was crawling on his hands and knees now. Stones covering the parking lot asphalt dug into his palms and knees as he scurried between running legs going around him. A woman with a pock-marked face kicked his leg and fell on top of him. Aaron looked over his shoulder as she pushed on his back and got back to her feet, continuing to run. That was when a heavy man's boot stomped on Aaron's left hand.

The pain felt like an army of hammers had crashed down on his knuckles. He screamed as loud as he could, but he still couldn't hear himself over the gunshots and screams of a thousand others.

Who's shooting? Who else has guns?

Aaron's hand probably only made the ground feel soft to the big man as he ran on without looking down. The boy curled into the fetal position and coddled his mangled hand to his chest. It was then that he spotted his brother, Brad, twenty yards away. He was crouched and huddled against their mother. Their father and Michael were pulling their weapons out of their duffel bags and ducking with every gunshot heard.

The last moments replayed in Aaron's mind like a completed jigsaw puzzle being shaken to pieces. He remembered that he'd been talking to his mother when there was an argument between two groups of men ahead in the line. The first gunshot became dozens within a heartbeat. As soon as the lines broke down and everyone ran for the front of the store, a truck rammed the vehicle barriers that kept cars out of the parking lot.

Aaron recalled watching an officer run towards two men from the first group of shooters and then watching him fall as the men sprayed bullets into the officer and everyone around him.

Michael cursed and shoved his way through runners to get to Aaron. They stayed low as more gunshots rang out, and Aaron tucked his face behind his big brother's shoulder. His hand throbbed with pain and felt like it was on fire. Looking down, he could see his middle finger was bent backward, and blood dripped down his arm.

"This way!" his father yelled.

Aaron didn't know where they ran, but he felt the crowd of people grow tighter around him. They all ran in the same direction. Shoulders pressed into his. It reminded Aaron of charging the front of the stage at a Breaking Benjamin, concert except everyone seemed to be wielding a gun.

Was everyone hiding them like us?

It wasn't until they bottlenecked through the front entryway that Aaron realized they were at the grocery store. Bodies compacted on all sides and someone's arm jabbed Aaron's hand, making him cry out. Being shoved through the metal doors and spilling out inside the front of the store felt like leaving a mosh pit for a race.

People fell over one another as they ran in every direction. They grabbed at each other's waistbands and feet, pulling them down so they couldn't beat them to the looting. Half the aisles of shelves were already empty, which surged a panic in everyone. This was Black Friday for food. It was a race, but with guns. This was a city without rules.

"Come on! Stay with me!" his father yelled over his shoulder. He led his family towards the bakery, where the fewest people had run. "This is our chance! Grab everything you can!"

Aaron's mother had found him through the chaos and hooked an arm over her youngest's shoulder like a mother bird shielding her hatchling from the rain. His father took a corner sharply around a set of empty shelves and smacked into a man running the opposite way. The other man had a soft body and the look of a father himself. The two men fell, and the boxes of chocolates and donuts the man carried spilled on the floor between them.

The soft-bodied man raised to his knees quickly. To do what, Aaron would never know because Aaron's father grunted a panicked sound and fired a round into the man's chest, sending him falling backward.

"Get—get the food!" Father huffed between breaths. His hands pawed at the torn boxes of sweets. "Put it in your bags!"

TWELVE

DERRICK HART

Derrick sat in his car with a line of orange cones flanking him on both sides. There was no way for a car to enter the road he blocked without driving on the curb or ramming his police car, which had the blue light activated. Still, he got the question.

A blue Toyota chose not to turn left or right at the intersection but drove straight, stopping a few feet ahead of Derrick's Charger. The driver, a skinny man with no shirt, exited the car and approached.

"Is the road closed?" he asked.

Derrick half rolled down his window and stared at the man, struggling to silence every smart-ass comment that bubbled to the top of his mind. "Yes."

"Well, I have to get through. I have to get to the other side of town." The man gestured behind Derrick with one hand while the other hung off his hips.

"You have to go around."

"How am I supposed to do that? I don't know any other way."

"You can't keep blocking the intersection with your car. You've got to move it and go figure it out." Derrick rolled his window up before the man could retort. The man finished his complaints without Derrick taking part in the conversation. He heard him through the closed window, yelling and cursing, before finally returning to his vehicle and aggressively driving away. Out of all the shitty jobs cops had to do, traffic control was the one Derrick hated the most.

At least we just have to block a road and not direct traffic.

Adams sat in the passenger seat, his head slumped against a balled-up winter jacket he used as a pillow. The man slept like he was in a coma. He had another twenty minutes before Derrick had to wake him up. Then it'd be Sergeant Bower's turn to sleep for two hours. Hopefully, by the time the rotation came back to Derrick's turn, he'd get some off time and be able to go home. He hadn't let his dog out since before he visited Alyssa the night before.

I'm going to have to figure something out for Ginger if this schedule keeps up, Derrick thought. *God, I can't imagine being a single parent right now...*

The talk radio had kept him awake for the past hours, but it was repeating itself now, discussing the passage of the National Security Act and how likely law enforcement and honorably discharged soldiers are to sign the Honor Bound contracts. Before that, they rehashed the legality of National Guardsmen shooting unarmed civilians who were infected with the virus, and the strong case for civil litigation against the federal government on behalf of the infected people's families. Before that, they discussed receiving the first unconfirmed reports of cases of the infection in southern Georgia and Alabama.

This virus wasn't like other viruses. When you got sick, you didn't just cough and bleed until you fell down and died. The virus turned the infected mad, crazy with violence. They couldn't communicate. They couldn't stop themselves from attacking whoever was in front of them. Whether it was a cop or a soldier in front of them or a child, they attacked them all. The infection had effectively killed an entire state in a handful of days, and there was still so little they knew about it.

Where did it come from? Was this an act of terrorism? Is there a cure? Is this the end? Is this how we all die?

Derrick felt the itch of sleep pull on the corners of his eyelids, and he allowed the feeling to tease him. The talk radio became background noise and Adams' deep breaths became a lullaby Derrick could fall asleep to. Before he could jolt himself awake, the car police radio became alive with hurried shouts and strained voices.

"Shots fired, shots fired!"

"Over here! Shooter is over here!"

Derrick straightened and adjusted the volume knob as Adams was roused from his sleep.

"What's that?" he asked.

"I don't know," Derrick didn't have a laptop in his vehicle like the patrol cars did so he couldn't find where the officers were, he could only listen as the stressed dispatcher struggled to get a location and suspect description from the officers on scene.

"Get back! Get—they're charging inside! They're overrunning the supermarket!" one officer yelled into their radio.

"Which supermarket?!" Derrick yelled at his radio, unsure of which direction to drive. He leaned forward and looked down the block to the next intersection, where Sergeant Bower's Ford Explorer sat. The headlights stuttered on his SUV as he started the engine.

A moment later, the dispatcher got an address from an

officer and put it out to all airs as a shooting in progress. Derrick's Charger was already roaring to life as he took a left and turned on his emergency equipment.

"Take 14th Ave; they've got it shut down for us," Adams pointed to the intersection they approached.

Derrick took the corner hard and sped up through the turn as he tapped the sirens, switching between the yelping frequencies and the wailing. He glanced at the rear-view mirror and saw Sergeant Bower take the turn in his SUV.

"Officer down, officer down!" a panicked voice screamed on the car radio. They weren't far from the scene, but in a situation like this, seconds mattered.

"We've got multiple wounded inside the store–it–there's shooting in here!"

"Send—send medics—we need medics!"

"Son of a bitch," Derrick gritted his teeth as he floored the gas pedal and heard the engine whine as it picked up speed.

Adams pointed his rifle at the floorboard as he looped the single-point sling over his head and arm. Racking the operating rod back, he chambered a round, then used a finger to scrub the crusts of sleep out of the corner of his eyes.

"It's up here on the left," Adams called out.

His voice was louder than it needed to be. SWAT or not, they were still first responders on a scene with multiple gunshots. Neither Derrick nor Adams had ever shot anyone before, and they hadn't been shot at either. Today would be the first time for both.

"I see it."

Hundreds of people poured out of the parking lot into the street while cars crashed into another trying to get in. Derrick jammed his finger down on the siren as he bottomed out his charger on the curb and blocked the hole in the roadblocks so no more civilian vehicles could enter. Derrick and Adams' doors exploded open simultaneously as they exited with their rifles.

Sergeant Bower skidded to a halt behind them and sprinted to catch up to his men.

"Remember, it's just us," Bower said to Derrick and Adams. "Keep it tight."

"10-4," Adams replied after hesitating.

The parking lot was a sprawl of bodies. Dozens laid, crawled, and limped in different directions. The ones who weren't wounded sprinted for the supermarket building and jammed inside.

"Here! Over here!" Derrick saw a patrol officer waving them down. He stood over another patrol officer who was flat on his back.

"4SAM86 to dispatch," Derrick said into his radio, then forced himself to take a deep breath to calm his voice. "We're on the scene. Be advised we have multiple wounded civilians in the parking lot. Approximately twenty to twenty-five people, as well as an officer with critical injuries. Start multiple medics this way, have them stage for PD to secure the scene."

They had almost reached the patrolmen when Derrick heard a motor rumble behind them. He glanced over his shoulder and saw a pickup truck that had entered the parking lot before they arrived barreling towards their backside.

"Hey—hey! To the rear—stop!" Derrick shouted. He and Adams stopped beside one another and faced the truck as it accelerated for them.

Fifteen yards. Ten yards...

With rifles raised, Derrick's red dot optic reticle rested over top the driver's side of the windshield as he snapped the trigger back several times. Adams fired, too. Their bullets pelted the windshield and hood of the truck in rapid succession until the truck hooked to the side and idled to a crawl in the middle of the parking lot.

"Check it," Sarge yelled from ahead. His rifle scanned the crowd, covering them. Derrick jogged in front of Adams, who dipped his rifle so as not to laser him with the barrel. Derrick slung his rifle and drew his pistol as he jogged beside the truck and opened the passenger door. His handgun aimed inside the cab, Derrick saw the bloody, limp body of a gray-haired man with a bushy mustache wearing multiple bullet wounds to the head and chest.

"Derrick, the truck," Adams said as he jogged beside it. Derrick's eyes bounced to the front of the truck and saw it was idling towards a group of wounded civilians huddling over a dead body. Derrick leaped inside, grabbed the gearshift, and slammed it into park, rocking the vehicle to a halt. The driver tilted forward, then his forehead smacked into the steering wheel.

Derrick pulled on the suspect's shoulder, and he collapsed on the pavement outside the truck. Grabbing one of his pair of zip-cuffs attached to the back of his body armor, Derrick secured the driver's wrists behind his back.

Derrick and Adams caught up to Sarge as he reached the patrol officers.

"He's shot!" the panicked patrol officer screamed with wide, rookie eyes. "They shot him a bunch, like four times. Where's the ambulance? Where—"

"They're coming, brother. Back up," Sarge said, pushing the patrol officer to the side. Derrick took a knee beside the wounded patrol officer as Adams stood watch over them. 'Randle' the officer's name plate read. He was conscious, but blood spewed from his cheek.

He was shot in the face, Derrick grimaced.

It looked like the bullet hit his jaw and came out of his cheek. Derrick padded his palms across Randle's chest and arms, stopping to check his hands for more blood, searching for another wound. When he got to Randle's thigh, his palms came back soaked in red blood and Derrick heard Randle groan where he was shot.

Gunshots erupted from inside the store as handfuls of people came running out the door, carrying armfuls of food and supplies. "We've got to go," Sarge said over Derrick's shoulder.

"Hang on," Derrick said. Grabbing his tourniquet from the pouch on his chest, he circled it under Randle's thigh and worked it back and forth until it was wrapped high near his crotch. Cinching it tight to one side, he heard Randle gargle a cry of pain as he twisted the windlass several times, tightening the tourniquet on his leg until the wound stopped leaking blood.

"Go!" Derrick told Bower and Adams. "I'll catch up."

The two moved on with a purpose. Derrick unclipped his key remote for his Charger and extended his blood-soaked hand to Officer Randle's friend. The patrol officer's nameplate read *Miles*, and the boy's pale, wide-eyed expression made him look like a man half his age.

"Miles, take this—" Derrick shoved the key fob into his hands. The kid looked down at the bloody key fob in his hand, then back up at Derrick. "Hey—hey! Get him to that Charger and drive him to the hospital, now. Go!"

Derrick sprinted ahead and shouldered his rifle. He caught up with Sarge and Adams just as they stacked up outside the front door of the supermarket. Looking back, he saw Miles dragging Randle out of the hot zone towards the Charger. He couldn't worry about Randle or anything else right now.

Gunshots were competing with one another inside the store as people fled the entrance.

Derrick tucked against the wall behind Adams and squeezed his arm. Adams reached ahead to Bower and squeezed the back of Sarge's triceps, telling him they were set.

"4SAM80 to dispatch, give us the air; we're going inside," Sergeant Bower radioed.

THIRTEEN

DERRICK HART

Pushing inside the store, Sarge button hooked to the right, Adams crossed to the left, and Derrick followed Sarge to the right. Rifles were raised at the low ready. Derrick had cleared thousands of rooms and structures over his career and arrested hundreds of suspects, but nothing ever like this. This wasn't a room; it was a supermarket—a giant warehouse of aisles with no walls or door to put your back to for safety. They weren't looking for one or even a handful of suspects, instead, everyone they saw was a potential suspect.

The aisles were packed with bodies jostling each other as they scooped clean the already bare shelves. Employees, identified by their light blue polo shirts, screamed as they ducked between brawling men to flee past the three police officers. Trespassing, theft, vandalism, assault... the charges were endless. Derrick didn't give a shit about those crimes today. He had to triage his focus.

Gunshots rang out from unseen corners inside the store. Wives and fathers ran past Derrick with arms overflowing with canned goods as they eyed his badge cautiously. Derrick glanced at everyone's hands as they passed.

No gun. No gun...

"Contact, right!" Sarge called out. "Metro Police! Drop the gun, drop the gun!"

Derrick pivoted to the right, fanning to the left so Sarge wasn't between Derrick's rifle and the target. The suspect had a black pistol in his hand down by his side. He was a young, Hispanic man with a thin black mustache and shaky eyes. The boy's free hand gripped a grocery bag stretched to the limits with stolen goods.

"Drop it! Do it now! Now!" Derrick shouted.

His rifle trained at the man's feet so he could see if he raised the handgun or not.

Shoot or don't shoot?

Derrick could see the panic and indecision building behind the man's eyes. With a shake of his head, the suspect started to raise the gun and Derrick tensed. Then he saw the suspect raise the weapon to toss it to the ground. He also dropped the grocery bag and put his trembling hands up.

"On your knees," Bower ordered. "Get on—"

"Oh, shit!" another man yelled from the other side of the checkout lines. Two men had just left a nearby aisle. A white man with wild, unkempt hair and his overweight dark-skinned buddy dropped a large backpack that clinked with glass when it hit the floor. They both had handguns pointed in their direction before Derrick looked over. Firing a spray of bullets at the three cops, the two new suspects chewed their lips as they separated and overwhelmed the SWAT officers from their flanks.

Crouching down, Derrick slammed his shoulder into the cashier counter as he rolled to cover. Adams and Bower did the same behind the checkout counters on either side of him as bullets snapped into computer monitors and ricocheted off the tile floor. The Hispanic suspect, who had dropped his pistol, tried to run for the exit, but stray bullets thudded into his body, dropping him in front of Derrick.

Derrick crawled around the side into the checkout lane and saw the two shooters as they sidestepped toward the exit while shooting. Compacted into a small ball on his knees, Derrick peered slowly from behind cover and fired his rifle twice in quick succession. His bullets snapped the first suspect's shoulder back and paused the onslaught of fire from both of them.

Adams popped up and fired three more rounds from his rifle into the injured suspect's chest as Derrick tracked his red dot to the left to the second suspect. Squeezing the rifle tight to his shoulder, Derrick squeezed the trigger three times fast, causing red blotches to form across the suspect's sweaty t-shirt.

When both suspects went down, Sarge took the lead, charging at the men, and Adams followed. Gunshots continued to pop around the store as Derrick did a 360, checking for additional threats, and covering his teammates. Any person who was near the front of the store when their gunfight erupted had cut their losses and ran, causing a stampede at the exit. They left behind a dozen bodies that were battered, unconscious, or dead.

"Clear!" Sarge yelled as he zip-cuffed the two shooter's wrists behind their back. "You guys hit?"

"I'm good," Adams said with a shaky voice.

"10-4," Derrick said.

Sarge grabbed the suspects' handguns, ejected the magazines, and cleared the chambers before tossing the weapons on the top shelf of a nearby grocery shelf, out of sight. Derrick grabbed the Hispanic man's gun and did the same.

"Help... help me..." the Hispanic man groaned, reaching out for Derrick.

Derrick's eyes jetted down to the thick blood that soaked the man's shirt and streaked the white-tiled floor. "Just stay put, help is on the way. Here, put your hand here. Keep pressure on it."

A woman's screams overtook the store, drowning out the dozens of arguments and fights that were happening.

"Moving," Sarge said as he pressed forward toward the screams. Derrick and Adams followed. "T formation," Sarge called out with his eye hovering behind his rifle optic.

"10-4," Adams said after a brief hesitation, and he changed position so that his rifle faced the rear more than their direction of travel. The "T" formation was usually trained with at least a four-man team. Three shooters with their guns facing forward as they moved, while the fourth traveled behind, watching the rear for threats. But Adams understood Sarge's meaning and adopted the formation with him on the rear, while Derrick and Sarge watched the front.

Every person who popped out from an aisle with hands full of something made Derrick's heart leap and his stomach drop. "Get—get out of here!"

Derrick swiped his non-dominant hand behind him as he shoved the looters away from his field of vision. His adrenaline surged, making him hyper-vigilant and on edge. He was doing all he could to control his breathing.

The woman was in the produce section, or what used to be the produce section. Every item had been picked clean and taken by the hoarding crowd. All that remained were wilted lettuce leaves from a broken bag and a few squashed tomatoes that had their guts spilled across the tile floor. She was middle-aged and a mess of screams as she lay on top of a man whose face kissed the floor. A pool of blood grew around his head. She rocked back and forth, clinging to his shirt as she screamed like a siren. Sarge moved past the woman while Adams lingered behind, setting up a perimeter.

"Derrick," Sarge said without looking at him.

Derrick understood and crouched beside her. "Ma'am? Ma'am? Metro Police, ma'am. Let me see..." The back of the man's head had multiple holes that leaked into the pool of blood and brain matter.

This was an execution.

"Ma'am, you need to get out of here. Now, Ma'am—"

There was a ferocious battle of gunshots that exploded from the back side of the store, and Derrick ducked his upper body on top of the woman's back. He felt her hands reach up and grab the sleeves of his uniform as she hid beneath him.

"Moving," Sarge said as he and Adams pressed forward. Derrick gripped the woman's shoulders tightly and pulled her upright despite her protests. He didn't have time to be nice anymore.

"Go! Now!" Derrick ordered as he shoved the woman so hard she fell to her side. Her tear-filled eyes looked up in fear at Derrick. A smear of the man's blood was still wet on her cheek. "Fucking go!"

Derrick jabbed his left finger at her, and she scrambled to her feet, rounding the corner for the exit. Derrick turned, the image of her terrified eyes burning into his memory.

FOURTEEN

AARON VANDERKAMP

"Just leave it, honey. Just leave it!" Aaron's mother begged. Her eyes darted over Aaron's shoulders as people ran by them in every direction. When someone veered too close to the pair, Aaron stopped shoving boxes of chocolate bars and donuts into his backpack and his hand touched the silver pistol that lay beside the bag. He pointed it once at a man who tried to grab his backpack. The man fell backward when he saw the weapon, then he ran. Aaron's mother covered her ears and screamed, anticipating her son's gunshot, which never came.

The man who'd originally carried all the chocolates had gone quiet. He stopped groaning and moving before Aaron's father and brother ran ahead to get more food, but now the man didn't even twitch, either. He'd gone completely still. The gunshot wound to his chest bled very little, though.

A pair of men dressed in black with tear tattoos under their eyes ran from the back of the store. They carried no food or supplies, only two rifles. They looked more like they were hunting than looting. There was a couple on their knees near the vegetable island a few yards away. They scooped half-crushed tomatoes into a backpack. Their eyes focused down on their task. The couple was oblivious when the two men in black stopped behind them. One man aimed his rifle down the back of the man's head and fired three times.

Everyone screamed. Aaron's ears rang like a high-pitched bell. The two men left the woman who grieved over her man's body and snickered with each other as they jogged by Aaron and his mother. It was so random, so pointless.

Why kill him and not her? Why not kill me? Why kill any of them?

When Aaron's hearing returned, all he could hear was his mother's screams.

"Oh my god," his mother cried. "Oh my god, just leave it. We have to—we have to go."

Aaron didn't know what was going on. He couldn't think. Everything was loud. There was too much screaming. Every time a gun fired, his shoulders tensed and jumped. He just remembered his father's words.

"Get all that food in your bag! We're getting some more."

Aaron grabbed two donuts that had broken free from their box and instantly smashed them in his grip, then shoved them into his backpack. It took an extra minute to zip up his bag with only one hand. His injured hand was cradled to his chest. It felt like it was on fire even when it wasn't being knocked around.

"Come on," Aaron said, grabbing this pistol. His mother grabbed the backpack like it was an oversized stuffed animal and hugged it to her chest. It looked as though it took effort for her to peel her eyes away from the man her husband had killed.

Louder gunshots and deep-voiced shouts called from the front of the store behind them. His mother didn't protest when Aaron led her after his father to the back of the store. They hopped over the legs of the woman who was crying over a man surrounded by a pool of blood. Aaron slipped on a smear of juices from a crushed tomato and felt his mother palm his shoulder from behind.

I've got to find Dad. Find Dad. Find Dad.

The words repeated in his head as he held the pistol out in front of him like a flashlight. The silver metal wobbled as he scanned each aisle he passed. Three men wrestled over each other. Next aisle, a woman with her hair in a ponytail hopped on her tippy toes, trying to get a large can of food out of a taller man's hand.

"Aaron! Over here!" Brad peeked his head out the back of a middle aisle. Michael and their father were on their knees, crowded around a bottom shelf that had stacks of soup shoved to the back and hidden away from anyone who was standing.

"It's a fucking gold mine," his father announced as he stuffed his duffel bag nearly full. There was a wildness in his father's eyes that gave Aaron pause. It was the release of his extreme competitiveness mixed with a primal excitement of survival. His father was going to win, no matter what.

"Gimme your bag. Nancy, give me it!" his father yelled.

A group of five men appeared at the front of the aisle. They wore baggy black clothes and had tattoos scattered over their arms and faces, which made Aaron think they were part of some gang. But it was the mean-looking guns in their hands that caught his eyes—long and short guns that looked like machine guns from the movies. Aaron recognized the two in the back with tear-drop tattoos under their eyes.

"Hey!" Michael yelled. He stood with his rifle in one hand as he faced the five men.

Aaron thought about yelling something. He wanted to warn his brother before it was too late, but his voice didn't work and shooting started before he could breathe. The explosion of gunfire was like a tornado of shrapnel. Bullets decimated the shelving and wooden end-caps that once held items on special sales. Pieces of plastic and chunks of debris rained down on his family as they crawled, rolled, and kicked their way out of the aisle. Aaron didn't see if his brother got any of them when he started shooting, but he knew Michael was shot badly without even looking.

His mother helped pull Aaron behind an island of shelves in the back of the store near the meat department.

"Mom, you're bleeding!" Aaron shouted when he saw the red leaking from her arm. The backpack fell from her arms as his mother seemed to feel the pain of the wound from him pointing it out.

She released a heart-wrenching scream as she clutched her shoulder, but the shooting had returned. His father and Brad retreated behind the meat counter, firing on the aisle they came from, and Aaron saw the same figures dressed in black appear at the mouth of the aisle.

But Michael isn't there. Where is Michael?!

"Run. Mom run!"

Aaron shoved his mother's back and forced her towards the meat counter. Bullets whizzed overhead and snapped at their feet. Glass along the wall shattered as they ducked away from the attacker's shots and snuck behind the meat counter. His father and brother went straight through the double doors into a warehouse area, but how close the bullets were hitting made Aaron and his mother dive left behind the counter to the left. They crawled backward toward a kitchen area.

A black blur suddenly appeared over the butcher counter. One attacker had jumped and fallen on his shoulder hard. By the time the man in black scrambled to his knees and had his gun in his hands, Aaron had his pistol aimed at the man's face and pulled the trigger.

FIFTEEN

DERRICK HART

"Hey, hey! Leave them, Adams!" Bower shouted.

Adams was hunched over a woman and two teenagers piled in the back corner of the store. There was a fight in Adams' body as he stuttered to separate from them. The three women seemed alive, but they all appeared shot, too. Derrick jogged to catch up as Adams and Bower disappeared around the corner to the back of the store.

Derrick heard the thunder of gunfire and took the corner with his rifle raised. He didn't have eyes on Bower, but Adams lay in the center of the floor with blood coming from the side of his head.

"Shit!"

Derrick saw one man dressed in black move to charge where Adams lay. Firing in quick succession, Derrick stopped the man in his tracks, reversed his run, and drove the man. He leaped over the butcher's counter, and there were more gunshots from behind there.

Snatching one of Adams' shoulder straps to his body armor, Derrick grunted as he dragged his friend's body into one aisle and left a streak of crimson blood behind. Adams' lips shook as he gasped for air and pushed it out in strange, momentary bursts. His body was limp and not moving.

Put it away, Derrick. Compartmentalize and prioritize. Finish the fight.

Gunfire sounded from every direction. Tattooed men wearing black shot from the middle aisles, exchanging fire with multiple shooters behind the butcher's counter.

Shit. We walked right into the middle of two groups fighting.

He couldn't get into the fight from where he had dragged Adams. There was no good angle, and besides, he would just be drawing fire towards the kid who couldn't defend himself. Gritting his teeth, he peeked around the corner and saw a metal fridge about ten yards ahead.

Bullets battered the floor and walls as Derrick fired haphazardly in the enemy's direction and dove behind the long, open-top freezer in the middle of the floor. He continued crawling from where he slid and rounded the opposite side of the freezer.

There was a certain point at which the human body could only register so much information at once, and he was nearing his limit. The sheer amount of chaos, deafening sounds, and destruction happening numbed him, moving his baseline for stress up to ten. The shock of being shot at was gone. The adrenaline rush of firing his weapon had passed. He acted in the moment now. It was time to win the fight.

Raised to a knee, Derrick peered from the side of the freezer he hid behind and saw two figures wearing baggy clothes and firing Uzi-style sub-machine guns toward the suspects hidden behind the butcher counter. Derrick rested the reticle of his red dot optic on the first man's temple and fired a single round, dropping him instantly. The second man turned, spraying 9mm rounds across the display in front of him before

Derrick reoriented his rifle and depressed the trigger three times. The bullet impacts made an oblong triangle in the second man's chest and collapsed him as he tried to flee.

Instead of silence after the two men were stopped, the gunfight continued between two parties. A chaotic barrage of multiple guns from behind the butcher counter and the patient-controlled burst of a lone rifle.

Sarge is still in the fight.

Touching the volume of his radio, he realized the thing got turned off during his maneuvering and clicked it back on.

When Sarge's gunfire stopped, he heard a familiar voice in his earpiece, "Derrick, you up?"

Derrick felt a thrill in his chest at the sound of Bower's voice and the pang of guilt, wondering how long the man had been looking for him. He keyed the mic attached to his chest, and whispered, "10-4, I'm right side, by the freezer thing."

"What about the guys in black? They're an aisle over from me," Bower breathed heavily.

"Took down two, I don't see anymore. Watch your six in case they've circled around."

"Copy. You got an angle?"

Derrick had already shot from the right side of the freezer, so he slowly peeked over top to get a second look at the butcher's counter. When he did, he saw two barrels that were waiting for him. They readjusted and opened fire.

"Negative, not a good one." Derrick panted into his radio. "Looks like at least two shooters behind the counter."

"Direct," Sarge keyed. "I've got a pretty good view from my spot. I can cover."

"10-4, hold what you got. I'm going to move right of the butcher entrance, then toss a bang."

"I'll cover you into position."

"10-4," Derrick whispered and took a deep breath. Tactically reloading, he swapped out his rifle magazine for a fresh mag and stowed the half-empty mag in his back pocket. "On you."

After an interval, Sarge opened fire on the two suspects, sending them into hiding, briefly. Derrick pushed off, running towards the wall of fridges that line the wall beside the butcher counter. Next to the countertop, there was a narrow passageway for employees to enter. Once through, it looked like there was a kitchen area to the left and double doors that led to the warehouse straight back. Derrick saddled beside the passageway as Sarge's covering fire tapered off.

"Fuck you!" a gravel-voiced suspect shouted as he returned fire in Sarge's direction. Then the suspect turned his fire to the freezer Derrick had once hidden behind.

They didn't see me move. They think I'm still by the freezer.

Removing a stun grenade from his chest rig, Derrick briefly released the grip of his rifle to yank the pin off the grenade before he tossed it into the mouth of the narrow passage. Averting his eyes, he shouldered his rifle and subconsciously counted the handful of seconds until detonation.

This was Derrick's chance to take the fight to them for a change.

The concussive *boom* vibrated the floors and knocked three of the freezer doors Derrick hid in front of open. Rifle up and scanning for threats, Derrick button-hooked into the passage as smoke from the charge still lingered in the air.

The first suspect was on his back with one hand covering his eyes and his rifle aimed conspicuously up at Derrick's position. Derrick lowered his barrel to the man's chest and squeezed the trigger three times in a row. The bullets cut up his center with the last of the three impacting in his throat. There was another body on the ground dressed in black that didn't move, and two other figures that stumbled in different directions. One headed left toward the kitchen, and another was going straight back to the warehouse.

Derrick strafed to the side, his red dot chasing the figure that went left.

Sarge's gunfire behind him startled him.

"On your six!" Sarge announced as he fired into the double warehouse doors. Derrick couldn't turn. Whoever was in the kitchen area to the left stuck a silver pistol around the corner and fired blindly in Derrick's face.

Derrick felt a stinging pain in his chest where one round pounded his armor. Clenching his teeth, Derrick did the only thing he could do. Move forward. Jerking the rifle trigger back, he fired at the arm stuck out from behind the wall until *click*— his rifle locked back empty.

No time, Derrick thought.

His mind had left behind tactics the moment he felt the sting of the bullet that hit his center armor plate. Rage mixed with adrenaline pushed him forward as he dropped his rifle, letting the sling catch it, and drew his sidearm from his drop holster on his thigh.

Derrick's right hand found the grip of his Glock 17 as his left hand snatched the wrist of the hand sticking out from behind the wall with a pistol. With a snarl, he forced the suspect's arm up in the air and rounded the corner with his own pistol tucked in a retention position at his side. Jerking the trigger back from point-blank range, Derrick fired multiple rounds into the suspect's belly until the gun fell from the suspect's fingers.

The man collapsed at Derrick's feet as Derrick's eyes came into focus. The youthful look on the suspect's face was full of pain and fear. He was a teenager. A kid...

"No!" a woman's voice shrieked and Derrick's mind broke free of the sight of the juvenile. A woman dashed out from deeper inside the kitchen, ignoring Derrick and his pistol trained on her as she fell on top of the boy.

No weapon. She has no weapon, he reminded himself.

She cried and grabbed at what looked to be her son. Derrick snatched the pistol from the floor so she couldn't grab it.

The double doors of the warehouse opened, and Derrick quickly pivoted, pointing his pistol before realizing it was Sergeant Bowers.

"Blue, blue ..." Bowers said.

"Shit," Derrick cursed, lowering his weapon.

"Back warehouse is clear," Sarge said.

"I'm clear," Derrick sighed, eyeing that there were no more places for suspects to hide in the kitchen.

Bower looked down and saw the mother comforting her dead son. "Shit, another kid."

SIXTEEN

DERRICK HART

Feet pattered the aisles of the grocery store as the cavalry arrived. At first, there were a handful of patrol officers, then dozens flooded the store. Derrick directed them to finish clearing the remaining corners of the building, but doubted anyone was left after their protracted gunfight.

Derrick's eyes tracked across the faces of the dead and dying suspects behind the meat counter as patrol officers handcuffed them and began first aid. The teenager in the warehouse that Bower shot. The teenager Derrick shot. None of them would survive. He would later learn that they were brothers, and that the one he'd shot was the youngest of three. All dead. An entire family wiped off the face of the planet over food. All except the mother, who only suffered a shoulder wound. Derrick last saw her being escorted to a patrol car whispering prayers to herself.

Derrick found Sarge kneeling over Adams' body. Adams' eyes were stuck open in a perpetual stare at nothing. The rifle rounds he was shot with had cut into his belly and throat.

Derrick took a knee with his sergeant and joined him in a prayer, but with so many bodies surrounding them, Derrick wondered if anyone listened.

The next minutes moved by in a blur. Officers that flooded the store had set up a perimeter and were triaging the wounded. Protesters delayed the ambulances downtown, so only one medic arrived. They packed it with four women and three men all suffering potentially survivable gunshot wounds. A woman with blood on her face approached Derrick while he stood in the parking lot. He was lost in the shock of the moment and spoke to her on autopilot, not recalling what she said by the time she left.

Derrick had never shot anyone before. This wasn't just another day for him. He knew the SOP (Standard Operating Procedure) for any officer-involved shooting was for the officer to be transferred to administrative leave while an investigation was completed. A field captain in passing had already told Derrick that was not happening.

With officers quitting the department and fleeing the city left and right, they could not spare any officer from the field. Derrick was in a daze, leaning against the back bumper of some patrol officer's cruiser. Dead bodies littered the parking lot as officers cordoned off the area.

ALEA, the Alabama Law Enforcement Agency, which typically investigated officer-involved shootings, would not be investigating the shooting. Shootings were happening too frequently, and too many agents had fled the state already.

No one's going to tell me if this was a justified move or not. No one to tell me if I did the right thing.

The face of the juvenile he'd shot appeared in his mind, followed by the screams of his mother. Derrick looked down at his hands and saw the dried smears of blood on his palms. He didn't know who it belonged to. It could have been one of ten different people killed. Remembering his own wound from an hour ago, now, Derrick lifted his own armor and palpated his chest where it had hit. He winced at a tender spot, but found no blood. The armor had stopped the bullet.

Loud diesel engines gasped and roared as they changed gears. Tan and camouflage Humvees and military vehicles streamed into the city in a never-ending column.

The National Guard had arrived. The size and sheer number of vehicles marked their established authority, relieving the police department. What should have felt like relief appeared more like a noose being fitted around Derrick's neck as he watched two dozen of the vehicles surround the parking lot and all the officers inside it.

Lost in a stare at the road, Derrick didn't even realize Sergeant Bower had approached him. They shared an exhausted look but said no words. The silence hung between them, filling the void of emotions they did not communicate. Bower unstrapped his body armor slowly, then pulled the heavy plate vest off from over his head. Setting the armor down on the trunk of the patrol car, he patted Derrick's shoulder one last time.

"You alright?" Sarge asked.

"You hear about the patrol officer? The one shot in the parking lot? Randle, I think?" Derrick asked.

"I don't know," Bower said. "I guess there were a few officers hit. I heard a couple didn't make it."

Derrick clenched his teeth to keep any emotions from spilling out.

"You know if Adams had any family in town?" Bower asked.

Derrick shook his head. "No, I think his family was from Arkansas."

"I'll call them from the road. Might get better reception outside the city."

Derrick looked at him without judgment and gave his sergeant a gentle smile.

"You gotta do what's right for your family, Derrick," Bower said after a long pause. "Protect those you care about. Protect yourself and your own."

Sergeant Bower handed Derrick Tom and Jeff's badges, then removed his own from his uniform and placed it in Derrick's hand. The two men hugged each other with a pat on the back, and Bower squeezed Derrick's shoulder before he walked to his SUV.

"Hey, Sarge!" Derrick called after him, and Bower paused, looking back. "If I were in your shoes with the kids and family, I'd do the same. Just wanted you to know that."

Bower gave a sad smile and nodded. "You can't save them all... remember that. Everyone has to draw the line somewhere, Hart. You can't save them all..."

When he watched his sergeant drive away, he realized he was now the only SWAT team member left in Birmingham.

Maybe the only one that can't take a hint.

And for the briefest of moments, he entertained the idea of getting in a patrol car and driving as far and as fast north as he could. He'd get to his best friend's place and stay with him and his wife.

And then?

Derrick felt a vibration in his breast pocket that seemed continuous. Taking out his cell phone, he saw he was in the middle of a data dump of news updates, text messages, and app alerts.

Derrick rolled the dice, found 'Brandon Armstrong' on his phone, and dialed his number. The odds were in his favor today, as the phone rang for several seconds before his best friend answered.

"It's about time, you shit-head," Brandon answered the phone. "I called your fucking ass two days ago. Where you been?"

He smiled, covering his eyes as he pinched the bridge of his nose between his thumb and forefinger. Derrick was glad he answered.

"Derrick?" Brandon said.

Derrick cleared his throat, "Hey asshole," he smiled.

"You enjoying Armageddon down there?"

"You know it. Just a party from start to finish."

Derrick had never served in the military, but while he was at college, Brandon served for six years in the U.S. Army as a Ranger and was deployed multiple times overseas. After his time in the Army, Brandon settled down with his wife in her home city of Nashville, Tennessee to do the 'family thing' as he'd put it.

"Yeah, looks that way on the news. How you holding up down there? Is it a shit show?" Brandon asked.

Derrick surveyed the scene of patrol officers securing the parking lot of dead bodies sprawled across the pavement. The news reporters were arriving and lining up to get their B-roll for the six o'clock news. The reporters would count the number of dead and hope there were enough to go national.

"It's... it was a shit show."

"I bet. Some asshole here last night during one of the riots threw a goddam Molotov cocktail into my yard, like what the fuck?"

"You guys okay?" Derrick asked.

"No, I'm not okay. I've got a fucking huge ass burned dirt patch in the middle of my lawn now!" Brandon yelled, and

Derrick couldn't help but snicker a laugh. "I'd have drowned that fucker in gasoline if I saw it happen."

There was a long pause before Derrick finally spoke.

"There was a run on a supermarket down here."

"When?"

"Just now," Derrick hesitated. "I, um, I shot some suspects. I killed them, I think. I don't know. I haven't heard yet."

"Damn, son," Brandon said quickly. "Sounds like you earned your paycheck today."

Derrick rolled his eyes and released a long sigh. The violent side of life always seemed to come easier for Brandon. He had killed as a soldier many times during his career. Derrick always had Brandon tell him about the situations so he could mentally prepare himself for the day he had to pull the trigger. He hadn't decided if he was prepared for it today or not.

"Yeah..." was all Derrick said.

"Listen, man, was it a good shoot? Did any bullets go down range and hit anything that didn't deserve it?"

Derrick ran through the brief minutes of the shooting that had felt like hours in his head. "It was a good shoot, I think."

"I didn't even have to ask, I know it was a good shoot, cause I've known your fugly-ass too long," Brandon said. "I know this type of shit isn't your thing, but I also know you're a squared-away, too. Forget all the bullshit and what people say. You saved lives today, you didn't take them."

Derrick nodded and took a deep breath. The shocked expression of the teenager he killed flashed before his eyes when he blinked.

"Besides, won't be too long and I might be out there with you soon."

"What'd you mean?"

"You see they passed Honor Bound shit? Just a revamped

name for the draft. Anyway, I re-upped. Just signed the papers. Can't let you have all the fun down there."

Derrick felt a twist in his gut. He knew if anyone was built for dealing with this shit, it was Brandon, but he also knew he didn't want his friend walking into this buzz-saw of a mess. "Karen must love that idea."

Brandon laughed, "She keeps threatening to divorce me, but I know her ways. She's all bark and no bite."

"Listen," Derrick said, "Brandon, this shit is going from bad to worse. I don't know if the news is just hyping this crap, or if it's really going to be a freaking zombie apocalypse, but don't stray so far that you can't come back, you know what I mean?"

"Hey, I don't see you running away from Birmingham with your tail between your legs," Brandon joked.

Derrick thought about Sergeant Bower and instinctively looked where his SUV was once parked. *You can't save them all.*

"No bullshit, though," Derrick said. "If you get word that this shit is turning from just a bad day into the end of the world, you let me know. And I'll do the same."

"Will do, brother," Brandon said, then added with a grin in his voice. "We can all go fuck off in Montana and grow beards. You and I can sit back and listen to Alyssa and Karen bitch at each other."

Derrick snickered and ended the conversation before Brandon asked any questions about Alyssa and he had to lie. He still hadn't told him about the failed proposal from a month ago. Derrick didn't know if he was more embarrassed by the rejection or hoping that she would change her mind and marry him.

And want to marry me...

"Hey, I gotta go," Derrick said. "Stay safe and don't be too much of an idiot out there, okay?"

"You'd be an idiot to believe any promise made by an idiot," Brandon said. "You keep alive, bitch, yeah?"

"You got it, asshole," Derrick said.

"Remember... Valhalla waits for no one."

"Valhalla waits for no one," Derrick hung up the phone after reciting their saying from childhood that had stuck with them all these years later.

Derrick got a ride from a patrol officer to the emergency room where Officer Miles had driven his Charger and left it hastily parked in an ambulance zone. Using his spare key, he opened his passenger door and saw the dried blood painted on the door, seat, and front dashboard. He didn't know how long he was lost in a stare at the massacre of a scene, but he awoke when his phone started vibrating again. Pulling it out, he saw the name that tied his belly into knots.

"Hey, Alyssa," he answered.

"Oh, thank God! I've been calling you like a million times," she said in a hurry. "Are you okay?"

"Yeah, why?"

"I see you on the news, well, *saw* you. I don't know if this is live. You were at that riot downtown at that grocery store, right?"

"Yeah," he said.

"Jesus, it looks bad. They said officers died, and I couldn't get a hold of you, and then I saw you standing in the parking lot and..." Alyssa let out a deep breath. "Sorry, I was just worried."

"I'm fine, thanks," he said.

There was a pregnant pause that was filled with tension on Alyssa's side of the phone call. Like she wanted to say something but couldn't find the right words. Derrick gave her time.

"So, um, I talked to my parents about that thing—what you came here to talk about yesterday. The, um, Honor Bound contract. The legal arrangement you wanted to do?"

"Yeah," Derrick thoughtlessly touched the passenger seat of his Charger. It was sticky with blood.

"Well, if you're still sure you want to do it and you're planning on staying on as a cop regardless, I think we should do it. Let's get married."

The quiet snicker Derrick made to himself was more like a sorrowful laugh.

It only took the apocalypse for her to say 'yes.'

"Alright, I'll come get you after I find a judge. I've got to go, 'Lyss."

"Okay," Alyssa said. "I'll, um, talk to you later—uh, Derrick? Thanks."

Derrick hung up the phone without a reply. Slumping in the passenger seat of his vehicle, he listened to the police dispatcher on the radio put out call after call. She asked for more cars and advised a supervisor of a hundred and thirty-two pending calls. He was lost in a stare at his blood-stained boots. He thought about the past few days and how they'd blurred into one. Part of him wondered if the next few days would be the same. Or the rest of his life.

Will today be the line of demarcation for the next fifty years? The day I killed multiple suspects who were trying to kill me? When I killed a kid? The day my friend died.

Adams was a good guy. He wasn't careless, and he was a better shot than his killer was, that's for damn sure. He died because he was in the wrong place at the wrong time. Had Derrick been in his position and taken that corner, he would have been the one in the body bag right now. The young SWAT officer was so excited to stay and develop from the experience into a better operator. Derrick remembered how adamant Adams was the morning he brought Derrick coffee. How confident he was that he would stay in the crumbling violence of Birmingham rather than flee. Derrick couldn't help but wonder if Adams had known he would die today...

Would you have fled, Adams? Would you have still shown up for duty?

Derrick blinked, and it was as if his state of shock had decided to turn off then. The noise of fifty different conversations he had after the shooting struck him at once along with a headache. He buried his sweaty face in his palm and took a deep breath, slowly exhaling, and the noise disappeared, leaving only one voice.

"You, um, I don't know if—if you remember me," the woman mumbled. Derrick had been in a daze when she approached him after the shooting. He didn't recognize her then, but he did now, recalling her face. The hysteria was gone, but her husband's blotch of dried blood on her cheek was still there.

"You—you saved my life," the woman started to say, but a frown broke over her face, and she pursed her lips while fighting off tears that glistened her eyes. After a wet sniffle, she continued, her frown transformed into a sneer, "Those men. The ones dressed in black. They killed my—my husband. For nothing! We—we were on our knees not even looking. They ran by and shot him in the head. They shot him in the head and then laughed. They laughed!"

Despite the rage in her eyes, tears broke loose, bulleting down her cheeks as she shook her head. "Did you get them? Did you kill those men who killed my husband?"

Derrick had nodded, which was enough for the woman.

"Thank god... they won't hurt anyone else," she whispered and hugged him. "I'm alive because of you. Thank you."

Derrick remembered the conversation as if he watched a movie of himself and heard it for the first time. Suddenly, he realized why his mind was recalling this moment. Adam's death... the answer to Derrick's final question for him... it was all connected.

Had you known you'd die today, Adams, would you still have shown up for duty?

The answer bloomed from Derrick's chest like its roots were buried deep in his core.

Yes, because this is what we do.

EPILOGUE

Derrick Hart
Birmingham, AL

...Days Later...

Nothing was as terrible as the sound of a man crying. It was the whimper of a wounded animal dying in the street. A man crying was a foreign sound that, once heard, could not be forgotten, no matter how hard you tried. Especially when it came from one of these men. The sheepdogs who protected the sheep.

Officer Derrick Hart lay on his back in the dark roll call room, his fingers curled around the chain that held a pair of worn dog tags around his neck. He had never served in the military. The two pieces of metal were not to identify him as a soldier but instead were all he had to tie him to his best friend. It was a cheap toy made of thin metal and meant to be snapped free and lost days after a child received them for their birthday or a weekend trip to the toy store. The chain on Derrick's set had broken on more than one occasion during his childhood but he always replaced it with another.

Dozens of police officers lay around him on the musky carpet and pretended to sleep; pretending not to hear the whimpering in the front of the room. It had been nine days since the outbreak in Miami, and Derrick questioned how many hours he had slept since then.

How much sleep has anyone gotten? How do you sleep when horror movies become reality?

Sleep wasn't measured in days and nights for police officers anymore but in clumps of hours here or thirty minutes there. This made these precious minutes of peace that were being disrupted by the crying man all the more serious.

The infected were coming. Thousands of them, millions, perhaps. The Army National Guard was now in charge and refused to give estimates, but everyone knew the infected were running to Birmingham. They were coming to tear Derrick apart along with all those who remained in the city. The first of them would arrive today.

Turning the piece of metal over above his face, Derrick studied the drawings of two Viking warriors on one tag. Their tattooed, muscle-bound bodies were strapped with a heavy axe and the other a broadsword as tall as the man. The two warriors looked nothing like his best friend or himself, but Derrick had always pretended they did as a kid.

Two brothers clasping arms before battle.

The second of the two tags read a quote that Derrick must have repeated with his friend a thousand times. '*Valhalla waits for no one...*' Of all the times he had read that, today was the first time Derrick's stomach dropped as he weighed the meaning of those words. Because today he would see Valhalla.

Today is the day I die, he thought.

He twisted the bulky, Redband bracelet that was fastened on his right wrist, letting air reach the soggy flesh beneath it. His thumb rubbed across the barcode etchings along the metallic side of the bracelet. It was his government-imposed tether that all present in the room had agreed to wear for the sake of their loved ones. Something to ensure they didn't flee their duty.

The layer of dried sweat and grease coating his skin pulled every time he moved. His auburn hair was the only thing greasier than his unwashed flesh. The closest thing Derrick had to a shower in the past week was pouring cold water over his neck from a hose behind the precinct yesterday.

At least I think it was yesterday.

He had stopped noticing his body odor last week and was getting better at not noticing others too. Derrick had an unassuming way about him. At twenty-nine years old, he was of average height with plain looks and soft features. Few would guess he was a senior member of the Birmingham SWAT team. He didn't possess the swollen muscles or gaunt jawline that the TV shows demanded of those on the elite team of the police department. He never wanted to be a superhero. Ever since he was a child, Derrick had only sought normality, something that his childhood was not.

The muffled cries that jabbed at the quiet room came from a young man who stood by himself near the whiteboard. The board behind him was covered in old messages from supervisors, 'OT Mandates,' 'found pair of handcuffs in sergeant's office,' along with an officer's hastily scribbled comment, 'also make sure all of the suspect's cocaine is out of their pockets before booking them (Alex!).' Long gray tables and black plastic chairs were shoved to the edge of the dim room and stacked on top of each other to make floor space.

Shrouded in the shadow of a stack of chairs taller than him, the young man held his face in the palms of his hands as he cried. Derrick could sense the old-timers beside him growing perturbed with these audible emotions.

Derrick did his best to ignore the messy sobs and focused on the other officers around him. Most tried to sleep but, like Derrick, they were too restless as they rolled about on the thin carpet that felt more like they laid on concrete slabs. Leaving on just their black work pants and black undershirts, officers had stacked their uniform shirts, body armor, and gun belts beside them.

Everyone dealt with the tense moments during downtime differently. Some men mumbled prayers to themselves–barely audible whispers filled with pleas for God's protection. Others stared at pictures of their loved ones under the glow of their cellphone screens. They twisted the Redband bracelets on their wrists. At some point, every police officer had doubts about signing the suicide contract so their loved ones could escape the city. Even Derrick.

Alyssa's safe with her family... at least you could give her that, Derrick.

No one talked to one another. He couldn't blame them. Just like he didn't blame the young patrol officer for crying. At some point today, every man and woman in this room would allow their tears to consume them in the privacy of a bathroom stall or patrol car. It was inevitable. There was only one thing on everyone's mind, and no one wanted to say it out loud. As if staying silent might keep death at bay.

Derrick took his phone out of his breast pocket hoping to see a green notification from her. A missed call or text message, some sign that Alyssa was alive. That she was safe.

That Alyssa is thinking of me, Derrick thought. He immediately hated himself for thinking it. But alas, the top of the screen showed the same symbol it always did. *No signal.* The only reason Derrick still charged the damn thing was for the few times it connected to a Wi-Fi signal, he'd receive sporadic data dumps of news updates, text messages, and voicemails that had been suspended in limbo for hours or days. But as 'America's Last Stand,' a term coined by news channels, approached, even the Wi-Fi seemed sluggish.

Instead, Derrick just stared at the photo on his home screen. It was a year-old picture of Alyssa on her tippy toes kissing a blurry-eyed Derrick on the cheek after a long night of drinking. The picture always made him smile, not just because of the moment, but what had occurred just after. His best friend, Brandon, had snapped the picture as they waited for their rideshare from downtown Birmingham back to Derrick's house. Not two seconds after taking it Brandon vomited the pitcher of strawberry margarita he had inhaled an hour prior. The mess had covered the front of Brandon's cowboy boots that his wife had insisted he wear. Karen and Alyssa had spent the rest of the night chastising him for splattering on them, and Derrick had to hold his gut because he was laughing too hard. He was sure he still had a video of Brandon passed out in a bush in his backyard later that night.

Derrick's smile soured as the sobs of the patrolman grew louder. He was more than background noise at this point. The base in his voice rumbled, making officers who slept stir.

"Please god... Please..." The young officer's voice broke as he cried his prayer.

"Jesus Christ..." A heavyset officer to Derrick's right grumbled as he turned on his side. To be honest, Derrick didn't want to listen to this kid's tears, either. Deep down, he wanted this boy to man up and give everyone some much needed peace before they died. That was Derrick's exhaustion talking.

But how else should this patrolman act? The military that now fortified Birmingham with hardened defenses fit for a

Russian invasion gave the Birmingham Police updates on how far the infected swarms were from them. Three days. Two days. One... This rookie officer was tormented by videos of infected civilians tackling Florida police officers in fits of violence. Men and women stripped of their humanity as they growled and screamed like animals. An entire state lost in days. And now three more teetered on collapse.

Now, Birmingham was all that stood in the way of the infection spreading to the rest of the country. And the ETA of the amassing hordes of infected wasn't days anymore, but hours.

"Ah, for fuck's sake," Tommy spat. "Shut the fuck up!"

Derrick couldn't see Tommy in the darkroom but knew his grating, Jersey-accented voice anywhere. It was ironic he was the one silencing another since Tommy had spent his whole career being told to shut his overactive mouth.

"Oh god..." The crying officer's voice broke. "I don't want to die..."

"Are you kidding me..." a deep voice groaned from the back of the room.

"Shut up!" another officer echoed as exasperated gripes joined in.

Derrick felt a knot in his throat and another forming in his gut. He tried to ignore the heavy and obligatory pull he felt from within when duty called. It wasn't something Derrick could just turn off, no matter how much he wished he could. All he wanted to do was sleep, but he couldn't just sit back and listen to this rookie officer being berated.

"I'm sorry, I just—I can't," the young man tucked his arms into his chest. His hands covered his face as his cries turned to hysterical sobbing. The kind of crying he probably hadn't done in twenty years, since he was a little boy tucked in the safety of his mother's embrace.

"Look, you fucking pussy," Tommy's voice boomed, again. This time he was up and lumbering toward the front of the room with heavy steps. Tommy was a giant to most. His six-foot-four, two-hundred-and-fifty-pound frame only amplified his broad shoulders and pointed jaw. "I'll fuckn' kill you myself if you don't shut up." Tommy snatched the smaller officer up by his lapel making the boy's metal pins on his uniform clang against each other.

Tommy's voice was erratic and strained, a testament to the amount of stress they were all under after days of sleeplessness and nights of violent rioting. The infection might not have reached Birmingham yet, but the riots, looting, and surge in crime had plagued every major city in the United States for over a week now.

"In fact," Tommy pointed down to the young man's duty pistol in his holster, "why don't you take that gun into the men's room and fucking eat the muzzle like the rest of the pussy suicides, huh?"

"I-I'm, I just–" the boy stuttered.

Derrick scrambled to his feet, but his aching body didn't move nearly as fast as he thought it would. His feet were covered in blisters and sores from being on his feet for twenty hours a day for over a week, while his chest and arms were covered in undiscovered bruises from working the riot lines at night.

"Here, I'll fuckn' help you pull the trigger," Tommy spat, reaching for the boy's weapon. But a small figure appeared behind Tommy before Derrick intervened. She was shorter than both of the men. When she pushed between Tommy and the crying officer, she looked like a child trying to hold back her dad from a fight. Both her hands propped against Tommy's chest, failing to hold him at bay. That's why it was to everyone's surprise when Tommy collapsed onto the carpet like a chopped tree.

"I said, back the fuck off!" the woman shouted, pointing her finger down at Tommy. Derrick recognized the voice and in the gray hue of light, he was able to see Perry's familiar face.

Tommy writhed on the carpet. His hands clutched his groin, his knees pinched together like a cartoon character.

"You bitch!" Tommy fumed through gritted teeth. Like an angry bear, he clamored to his feet, marching towards Perry until he saw her Glock 19 half drawn out of the drop holster on her thigh. "Oh, you gonna shoot me now? Do it! Do me the favor, bitch!" Tommy held his arms wide open in a challenge as he stepped closer to her. His enormous wingspan made her seem even smaller.

The room became icy cold as the two stared each other down. In that hair of a second, the room wasn't full of police officers, but just a group of people at their wit's end. The anarchy that had spread through the country had finally found its way into the police precinct. Derrick broke from his trance long enough to muster as much of a commanding voice as he could despite his exhaustion. "Back off, Tommy!"

Tommy's eyes jolted over to Derrick, and he drew to a halt barely a yard from Perry. Tommy gave a measured snarl in Derrick's direction. Then, as if realizing where he was, did a brief survey of the dozens of officers staring at him.

With a final grunt, Tommy relented, turning away from Perry and the cowering patrolman "Whatever... fucking cunt."

Perry's eyes didn't leave Tommy until he fell back to his spot on the floor, his hand rubbing his wounded crotch. Her hand seated her Glock back in the holster and she gave a brief nod to Derrick, which he returned. Derrick hadn't realized Perry was in the room until then. He hadn't realized she was still in the city.

She was one of the few who still had her gear and uniform on, but unlike the patrolmen whose shirts and pants were black, Perry wore a baggy, forest green uniform that matched Derrick's. She also wore a heavy vest similar to the one Derrick had laid beside him. It was covered with filled magazine pouches across the chest and white lettering across the upper back panel that read, 'SWAT.'

"I'm sorry. I just, I need–" the young patrolman stuttered. His face was a mess of tears, snot, and shock from what had just happened.

"It's okay... it's okay... what's your name?" Officer Perry asked.

"Miles," he answered, wiping his nose with the back of his hand.

"Miles, my name is Perry," she said.

The barrel-chested patrolman beside Derrick rolled to his side with a labored sigh, "Would you get that coward out of–"

Before Derrick could even consider speaking, Perry snapped at him, "Shut up you fat fuck and go back to sleep."

The man growled something to himself but did as he was told.

Perry turned back to Miles and pulled him down into an embrace, petting his hair as his mother might have. "It'll be alright, take a deep breath. In and out, come on."

The officer followed her instructions through wet sniffles. After a moment she pulled away but held Miles' shoulders as she looked at him.

"Listen Miles. I need you to suck it the fuck up, okay?" she said, pulling his six-foot frame down to her shorter self. "You're a fuckin' police officer. You're built for this shit, otherwise, you wouldn't have that badge on your chest. The rules are the same out there. Bad guys chase civilians, and we chase bad guys, okay? There's people out there who aren't as strong as you, who are counting on you right now. And more importantly, everyone in this room is counting on you, and I'm one of them. It's easy to be a cop when nothing bad is happening, but it's what you do now that matters most, okay?"

Miles nodded, taking a deep breath. He wiped his eyes on the back of his forearm.

"Okay. Now go outside, get some water on your face, and come back. Get some rest, alright?" Perry gave him a nod. Miles left the room quickly with his head tucked low. Derrick saw a brief glare of Miles' wedding band catching the light as he passed.

It's falling apart. Everything is about to fall apart.

Derrick laid back down beside his gear and rubbed his greasy forehead. If the police were barely holding it together, the military couldn't be far behind.

And the virus isn't even in Birmingham, yet.

Derrick rolled to his side and tried to quiet his mind. With a deep breath, he allowed his body to release the tension and begin his fast descent into sleep. His fingers touched the rifle that lay beside him as the world faded into darkness and his muscles unclenched for the first time in days. His relaxed mind rested on thoughts of Alyssa and wondering what his girlfriend, or former girlfriend, was doing.

Before the warm embrace of sleep could envelop him, the hallway door smacked open against the wall, rattling the room to life. The cut of the bright setting sunlight from the summer day shone painfully across their eyes. The roar of thumping helicopter rotary blades filled the room.

"It's time. Everybody up!" Captain Elwood ordered. "They're here."

Continue reading the Calamity series today and follow the Rabid virus' path of destruction!

Calamity

Sam Winter

Two elite operators and best friends will use their tactical skills to fight through the collapse of society in order to save their loved ones.

What weapons, gear, and rations do they have? Whatever they can find.

Get The Book!
Calamity, Book 1
Calamity Series

JOIN SAM'S NEWSLETTER TODAY!
NO SPAM, JUST NEWS

Join Sam's Newsletter for updates on future releases and bonus content. You'll also receive a free e-book today!

www.officialsamwinter.com/newsletter

ABOUT THE AUTHOR

Sam Winter is an American author who enjoys creating gritty fiction. Calamity is Sam's debut series that reimagines the collapse of modern society from the very first minutes of disaster.

When he's not writing, Sam enjoys binge-watching epic shows online & exploring the world one adventure at a time. Sam currently resides in Michigan with his dog.

www.officialsamwinter.com

Get to know him better by following him on social media.

 facebook.com/justsamwinter

X x.com/justsamwinter

instagram.com/justsamwinter

www.ingramcontent.com/pod-product-compliance
Lightning Source LLC
Chambersburg PA
CBHW022032170626
46808CB00003B/1167